ENDURING COURAGE

BOOK THREE OF *THE VICTORS SERIES*

Mary Carroll

authorHOUSE®

AuthorHouse™
1663 Liberty Drive
Bloomington, IN 47403
www.authorhouse.com
Phone: 1 (800) 839-8640

Published by AuthorHouse 07/02/2020

ISBN: 978-1-7283-6627-2 (sc)
ISBN: 978-1-7283-6626-5 (e)

Library of Congress Control Number: 2020912209

Print information available on the last page.

Dedicated with Respect
and Gratitude to
Dr. Joseph Jemsek

~ ~ ~

I owe you my life.

A Note From the Author

Enduring Courage is a little bit different from the first two books in this series, as it endeavors to educate as well as entertain. While the characters and overall story remain a work of fiction, the medical information I have incorporated here is factual. It was gathered from various sources, which are referenced at the end of this book. These very real details are shared here in hopes of informing people and raising awareness about a highly controversial and all-too-often misunderstood disease.

The medical specialist in this novel, Doctor Jason Jensen, is not a real person. However, he is based on a real man, Doctor Joseph Jemsek, to whom this book is fondly dedicated. The details the character of Julie Chambers provides about her symptoms and the long quest for care are identical to the experiences I have endured personally. Just as Doctor Jensen proves vitally instrumental in turning Julie's life around, Doctor Jemsek was responsible for doing the same for me. He continues to do so for many others, sometimes at great personal cost, and I consider him to be a hero.

My dear reader, thank you so much for taking this journey with me! It has been a wonderful experience, and I am so grateful to everyone involved.

Mary Carroll

Chapter 1

Julie Chambers was finally acknowledging the truth she had been avoiding far too long. *I still haven't told Emily what's going on with me, and I know I need to, but it's never the right moment for us to have this conversation! There's always something else going on and some reason the timing isn't right. Now Emily is pregnant! That's incredible news, and I sure don't want to put a damper on that amazing event, so once more, **my** news must be delayed. There's constantly a wedding, an injury, an illness, a new job, a holiday…*

The doorbell rang and brought the model out of her reverie as she went to answer it. "Anderson Blair, I told you this wasn't necessary," she chastised. "You didn't need to cancel your own patient load to go with me today."

Putting a gentle hand on her arm, Julie's boyfriend responded, "Yes, you did tell me that, and **I** told **you** that I wasn't going to miss it. Didn't you believe me? You should know me by now."

Realizing she couldn't win this debate, and too drained to try very hard, Julie surrendered easily with a kiss on his cheek. "Yes, I believed you. I'm grateful to have you with me, of course. I just feel bad for your patients."

"That's my girl… always so concerned about everyone else's needs that you don't consider your own. That's one of the many things I love about you. It's not like I'm a brain surgeon, my dear. I'm a physical therapist, so there is a little bit of leeway for shuffling things around with my schedule. I only had one person booked today, and he was fine to move his appointment to tomorrow, so it's all worked out. Now stop worrying."

"Ok, Honey. Sounds like you have it all taken care of. I'm almost ready to go." The blonde sighed and went back to her room to put on her shoes. *I'm really tired today, both physically and mentally. My body and mind have been fighting this thing for so long, it's no wonder I'm exhausted.*

The pair of smiling faces in the framed photo on her dresser caught her eye. She picked up the picture of her parents and gazed at it lovingly. *I miss you guys! I know the volunteer work you're doing overseas is very important, and I've told you numerous times not to come home because of me, but sometimes I do selfishly wish you were here.* Julie put the frame back in its place and sat down on the edge of the bed. Maneuvering her feet into her shoes, another thought crossed her mind and took on a tangent.

I'm very worried about my career. I don't want people to forget who I am! Things were really gaining momentum before this craziness happened, but it's been slowly jeopardizing my dream ever since. My agent has been incredibly patient, but how much longer can that last? I need to schedule a time to touch base with her soon and chat.

*I just don't understand why it took so long for my symptoms to escalate! There's still so **much** about all this I don't know. Hopefully, today will be the first step toward changing that.*

With a courtesy knock on the open bedroom door, Anderson came in as Julie was struggling to tie her sneakers. "You've been in here awhile. Are you ok?" He knelt and completed the task for her, causing a tear of gratitude to slide down her cheek.

"I guess I'm as okay as I ever am," she mumbled. "I'm just… so… **tired**, Anderson."

He tenderly wiped away the tear and reminded her, "You're not alone, and you don't always have to do everything for yourself. We're in this together. Please remember that."

She took his hand and smiled her thanks, knowing if she tried to say anything, there would be a full-blown blubber fest, and there simply wasn't time for that right now. Julie leaned on Anderson for support in every sense as the couple headed to his car.

~~~

"Nick, did Julie seem… I don't know… less than enthusiastic about our news?" Emily Peterson was lying in bed rubbing her belly. Although her due date wasn't until August, she was already falling in love with the miracle baby growing inside her.

"I didn't notice anything like that," her husband responded, adjusting his tie as he looked in the mirror. "You're right, she wasn't overly zealous, but didn't you say she hasn't been feeling well? Maybe she was just distracted by that." Nick crossed the room and sat on the bed next to his wife. "You don't think she's jealous of this little one, do you?" he teased, putting one of his hands on her belly as well.

"Oh, no, it's nothing like that," Emily replied. "I don't know **what** it is, but it feels like something about her just isn't quite right. She was definitely distracted, like you said. We haven't had any real 'girl time' since the spa day you treated us to for my birthday. That was some time ago… maybe she's feeling like I don't have time for her or something."

"That could be," her husband agreed. "Hey, you can fix that! Give her a call today, make lunch plans for this week, reconnect." He gave her a kiss and stood to go.

"You look very handsome, husband," she complimented him with a grin.

"Thank you very much, wife," he replied with a formal bow. "So glad you approve. I can't go on live TV looking like a run-of-the-mill tatterdemalion."

"Like a **what**?" she laughed. "You made that up!"

"Oh, do you think so?" he quipped and raised his eyebrow as a challenge.

"I **know** so! That is **not** a real word!" she asserted.

He leaned toward her and lowered his voice. "Would you like to make a wager on that, Mrs. Peterson?"

*Knowing him, it **is** a real word and he's trying to trick me. Well, I'm not falling for it.* Instead she changed the subject. "Have I thanked you for doing the series of shows about Parkinson's disease?"

Nick laughed, "Only about a hundred times. Nice deflecting there, Sweetheart. That was several months ago!"

"I'm not deflecting! It was so successful, and instrumental in raising awareness and educating people. It meant a great deal to me and my parents that you did it."

"We actually still get feedback on it, even now. You're right, it was a big success! Maybe I will make it an annual event…" Nick took his phone out of his pocket and dictated, "Talk to Karen about having Parkinson's Awareness Month **every** May."

"You're amazing," Emily cooed.

"Nah, I just know what makes good television," Nick joked with a wink. With one more kiss for his wife he urged, "Call Julie. I'll see you tonight."

As soon as Nick left the room, Emily grabbed her phone and searched online for "tatterdemalion". *Well, look at that! It **is** a real word! It means 'a shabby, unkempt person'. Nick Peterson, you never cease to amaze me!*

While she had the phone in her hand, she decided to go ahead and call her best friend. *A girls' lunch is just what we need!* After three rings the voicemail picked up. Leaving a cheerful message, she nestled back into the covers to steal a few more moments before she had to get up and get ready for work.

~~~

Andrew Peters sat at the desk in his well-appointed office with a contented smile on his distinguished face. *I'm going to be a grandpa again! We never thought this could happen! If there's any justice in the world, all will go well and there will be no more tragedy in this family, only joy.* His daughter had made the big announcement over a week ago, but he and his wife, Meagan, were still over the moon about the miraculous news.

"Well, you certainly look happy this morning!" Josie greeted her boss cheerfully as she brought in some documents that required his attention. "In fact, you look a bit like the cat who ate the canary. Anything you want to share?"

5

Andrew was focused on the stack of papers his assistant handed him, but he replied with a grin, "You're very perceptive, Josie. Yes, actually, there is some **extremely exciting** news, and I suppose it is about time that it was revealed."

"Oh, this sounds big! What is it? I can hardly wait!" The staff here was like a family, so she was eager to be a part of whatever happiness had her boss smiling so much.

"I appreciate your enthusiasm, but you're going to have to wait a little longer," Andrew bantered.

"But you just said…" Josie protested.

Andrew held up a hand to silence her. "I said it's time this secret was revealed, but it isn't really my news to tell. It's my daughter's. Please go alert everyone that there will be a staff meeting as soon as Emily arrives."

Chapter 2

"Are you ready?" Anderson asked Julie as he helped her from the car.

"I'm ready to get answers, and get a plan in place, yes. I'm not sure if I'm quite ready for the implementation of it, though," she answered truthfully. "I wish I was more confident that this is the right thing to do."

"What do you want, a sign?" he said with a laugh, but she wasn't amused. "Sorry for that. Look, Doctor Michaels puts a lot of faith in this guy, and he wouldn't have referred you to him otherwise. It's going to be okay. You're strong, and you have a great support system," he assured her. Looking toward the building ahead, she took a deep breath, and the couple headed inside together.

This waiting area was larger and more crowded than the one at Doctor Michaels' office, and Julie briefly wondered if she would have another experience of her privacy being violated. If any of these patients scattered around the room recognized the model, they had the tact not to acknowledge it. She wasn't sure if that was a good or bad thing, considering her concerns about her career, but she was glad to check in without incident and sat down in a corner with Anderson to wait her turn.

After several minutes passed and the room began to clear out as other people were called to the back office, she started getting restless. She stood up and began looking around the lobby, and some of the framed items captured her attention.

There were the usual diplomas and awards seen displayed in many doctors' offices, and Julie silently read his name, even though she already knew it: *Doctor Jason Jensen*. She moved on to mull over some abstract artwork along one wall and noticed there was a beautiful piano in the corner. *That's different for a doctor's office. I wonder if he plays?* She would find out later that he, in fact, played quite well.

When she reached the two companion pieces near the receptionist's desk, she stopped in her tracks with a sharp intake of breath. *How did I miss these when I checked in? This is quite literally a sign... **two** of them!*

There in front of her were two beautifully matted and framed genealogy documents that showed the history of the doctor's first and last names.

Jason: Greek, meaning "Healer"
Jenson: Danish, meaning "Merciful"

~~~

"Good morning, Dad!" Emily poked her head into her father's office on the way to her own, intending to move along to her desk and get busy. His voice changed her plans.

"Emily!" he called out before she got too far away. "Come back in here, please."

"Sure, Dad, what's up? Do you need something?"

With a grin, he answered, "I think it's time."

She was lost. "Okay… time for…?"

Standing and walking out from behind his desk, Andrew put his arm around his daughter. "It's time to let the staff know that you're expecting."

"Oh!" She was clearly surprised. "Really? It's still early…"

"I didn't think of that. Would you prefer to wait until you're further along?" *After what happened the last time, I should have known she may not be ready.*

One look at her dad's face showed her how excited he was to share the news, and it wasn't yet settled how much longer he would be there before he fully retired. She knew he wanted to have the opportunity to enjoy all the good wishes from the employees while he could, and she wanted that for him, as well.

"You know what, Dad? I think you're on the right track. Let's tell them!" Slipping her hand in the crook of his arm, she asked, "How should we do it?"

"I was hoping you would be on board… I already have everyone waiting for us in the conference room. Believe me, they are an inquisitive bunch!"

The two of them walked into the meeting space chuckling and saw that it was filled to capacity with everyone from custodians to upper management officers. "Well, it sure looks like everyone's here!" Emily exclaimed.

Josie spoke up, "Word got around quickly that you had an announcement to make!"

I'm glad I went along, or this would have been embarrassing for Dad and me both!

"Thank you so much for this lovely outpouring of support… or curiosity, whichever it may be." Emily laughed and the staff groaned.

Someone near the back of the room joked, "Can't it be both?"

Another unidentified voice called out, "Stop stalling!"

With a deep breath, she decided not to make them wait any longer. "Okay, okay, so… the big news is… come this August… I'm going to have a baby!"

"Congratulations!"

"That's so exciting!"

"It's wonderful!"

"Oh, Emily! It's a miracle!"

"How does it feel, Grandpa?"

Not much work got done at AP Securities that day. Most of the employees had been there through the tragedy of Emily and Nick losing Sarah Beth, and the ones who hadn't were quickly brought up to speed. Everybody understood the significance of this revelation, and nobody was more keenly aware of it than the very eager mother-to-be.

~~~

"Did you talk to Julie?" Nick asked that evening as he and Emily were preparing dinner together in their spacious kitchen. They had decided on large salads with strips of chicken, and Nick was bringing the meat in from the grill.

"Not yet," his wife answered with concern in her voice. "I tried but got her voice mail when I called this morning. I left a message, but she hasn't called me back. I hope she's okay." She tore lettuce into two bowls as they talked.

Nick got out napkins and silverware and began to set up TV trays in the living room. With a smile he tried to encourage his wife. "Oh, I'm sure she's fine. She probably had a busy day and just hasn't had a chance to call yet."

Emily stopped mid-slice of the tomato in front of her and puzzled, "Busy doing what? She hasn't been working... she's not been feeling well... I don't understand. Why hasn't she told me what's going on, Nick?"

He stepped over to her and rubbed her shoulders. "How do you know that there's **anything** going on? Are you maybe overreacting a little bit?" With a kiss on her cheek, he poured two glasses of iced tea and added them to their trays.

"I don't think so, Honey," Emily called out so he could hear her from the other room. When he came back to the kitchen she continued. "Actually, I think I've been underreacting by not asking more questions of her lately."

"Sweetheart, I'm not sure if 'underreacting' is a word," Nick said, very seriously.

"Oh really? Kind of like I wasn't sure if 'tatterdemalion' was a word?" she countered.

"Right... and how did that turn out? I'll bet you looked it up before I was out of the driveway!" He laughed out loud because he knew he was right.

"Nick Peterson, you think you know everything!" She folded her arms and pouted.

"You're deflecting again, Sweetheart."

"I am not!" she defended. "I just get tired of... well, tired of..." She didn't want to admit it, so she was stalling.

Kissing the end of her nose, he asked, "What do you get tired of, My Love?"

"I get tired of you being right all the time," she admitted.

Taking her into his arms, he bantered, "It's not **all** the time. Besides, **you** are almost always right yourself... just not about 'underreacting' being a word."

Playfully pushing him away, she exclaimed, "Well, if 'overreacting' is a word, then 'underreacting' should be too!"

Nick grabbed his phone. "Let's look it up, shall we? Hey, how about that? You were right this time! See, we both have our moments!"

Emily did a barefoot dance around the kitchen with glee, taunting him. "I was right! I was right! You were wrong! I was right!"

The couple enjoyed their continued humor as they finished making dinner, then took the food in the living room to watch TV and relax while they ate. Somehow the subject of what was going on with Julie got set aside.

Chapter 3

The appointment with Doctor Jensen went well. When Julie showed the two ancestry certificates in the lobby to Anderson, she thought he may tell her she was being silly finding comfort in something like that. Instead, he agreed that knowing the doctor's name meant "Merciful Healer" was somehow reassuring.

Not long after that, a nurse called the couple to the back office. She checked Julie's weight, blood pressure and other vital signs, then escorted the two of them to a comfortable patient exam room. Once they were settled, Julie allowed herself to begin to feel a little more hopeful than she had in quite some time.

When Doctor Jensen joined them in the room and introduced himself with a warm handshake and inviting smile, she was instantly comforted by his demeanor. "It's very nice to meet you, Miss Chambers," he greeted as he took a seat across from his new patient.

"Please, call me Julie," she asked. "I have the impression we're going to be seeing a lot of each other, so there's no need to be formal." She managed a weak smile at the physician then lowered her head and studied her uncharacteristically unpainted fingernails. *Wow, I could really use a manicure.*

Where did that come from? What a random thing to be thinking about right now!

Sensing how nervous she still was, Anderson reached over and wrapped one of her hands comfortingly in his. At his touch, the blonde realized the room had grown quiet in the few moments while she was distracted. She squeezed a silent *thank you* in her boyfriend's grip and returned her attention to the specialist in front of her.

"Sorry about that, Doctor Jensen," she apologized. "My mind wanders so easily since all of this."

"I totally understand, Julie," he replied with compassion. "That's part of it, unfortunately, but I'm used to it. Don't worry, I don't take it personally!" They all laughed, and it helped relieve her tension.

"So, where would you like to start today?" Doctor Jensen neatly stacked the pile of papers in front of him that made up her medical history so far. "Doctor Michaels has forwarded me copies of all of his office notes and test results from your visits with him, so I'm up to speed on your case from a medical standpoint."

It's so bizarre to me that I would have a medical chart that large, and we're just getting started. Before this happened, I never needed doctors for anything other than annual routine physicals and the occasional sore throat. I'm still young and have always been so healthy, it's surreal to think those records are mine! Realizing she had zoned out again, Julie shook her head to clear the mental cobwebs and tried to focus her attention on the matter at hand.

"For now," the specialist was saying, "I'm concerned with how you are feeling mentally and emotionally about the situation. I'd like us to talk about your thoughts and what your questions are, that sort of thing."

This guy is really supportive. Since I've not had the need to know a lot of doctors in my life, I don't have much of a comparison other than Doctor Michaels, who's great. Doctor Jensen is so kind and caring. That's bound to make things a little less scary going forward.

"Mostly I guess I would say I'm feeling confused." Julie wasn't sure what other word she could use that would better describe her state of mind.

"That's a reasonable answer. There's a lot going on and I'm sure you have many concerns." The doctor waited for his patient to continue.

"Yes, I sure do. I'll be honest with you, Doctor Jensen, it's very difficult for me to talk openly about all of this. I tend to keep it pent up, because discussing it makes me feel overwhelmed, and then that upsets me. It's not pleasant."

"I'm used to that, too, Julie. You've been through a lot already. You don't understand what's happening to you or what comes next. Naturally, that would be disturbing. But I need to have this conversation with you to help you get better."

With a heavy sigh, she agreed. "I know. I'm just realizing I'm not feeling quite as prepared for it as I hoped I would at this point."

"Tell you what. Let's not rush it. How about we take a short break for you to gather your thoughts, then come back and start at the beginning, and you tell me your story. I will listen and make some notes, then help address your questions. By the time we're done, hopefully things will be clearer for you."

Gosh, he makes it sound so easy.

~~~

"What do you think?" Anderson asked as he handed Julie a paper cup of water from the fountain in the hall outside the exam room. "I know we're still getting to know him, but do you feel comfortable with Doctor Jensen so far?"

Accepting the cool liquid gratefully, she took a sip then answered, "Oh, yes, he has put me more at ease. He's genuinely nice and seems to have a great deal of patience and understanding. I'm just not… I don't know if…" Her voice trailed off and she drained the rest of the water.

"What's wrong? You don't know what?" her boyfriend coaxed.

Sighing, Julie replied, "I don't know if I can rehash all the details again, Babe. It upsets me and I get so flustered. You **know** that." With more force than was necessary, she crumpled the paper cup and hurled it into a handy trash can with a loud thud. The nurse at a nearby desk looked up at the noise and the blonde shrugged an attempt at a silent apology. The kind caretaker nodded her acceptance with a smile and returned her attention to the chart in front of her.

Anderson filled another cup with water for his girl then guided her back into the exam room. He quietly closed the door and sat the water down on the desk so it would be close by if she needed it. Then he took her in his arms and they simply stood there holding each other quietly for a few minutes.

When he finally stepped back, he assured her, "I know the next few minutes won't be easy. It's difficult to bring up everything you've been through and relay the details, and I realize it makes you uncomfortable."

"Uncomfortable? That's an understatement. I don't even understand **why** it upsets me so much, but it does." Julie's voice was trembling.

"It upsets you because it brings up bad experiences, Honey. As you and the doctor said, you have been through a lot with this thing. Heck, what you've dealt with would have destroyed many people."

With an emotional catch in her throat, she admitted, "There have been many times I thought it would destroy **me**."

He hugged her again, then encouraged, "I know. But you are **strong**, and you've never let this beat you. That's another one of the things I love so much about you."

Anderson's support is such a blessing. Meeting him has changed my life! I wish I could tell him all the things in my heart, but I'm emotional enough already. I can't go down that road right now!

When she didn't respond, he respected her silence and continued. "It's going to be okay. Remember a few things. First, this doctor has met with people just like you many times, and he is well aware of the emotional stress you're under. Second, it's necessary for your treatment for you to relay the details, so he can create the best plan for you, and we can work together to get you better. And third, you're not alone. I'm right here with you." He kissed her on the forehead just as the doctor knocked on the door and came back into the room.

"Okay, Julie, are you ready to sit down and chat?" Doctor Jensen began as they all took their seats.

She looked at Anderson once more, hoping to somehow draw strength from his smile. In response to the doctor's question, she only nodded.

"Great. Start with telling me about when you first began to have symptoms, or even go back to when you were bitten by the tick, if you know that."

I can do this. Millions of people all over the world have Lyme disease, just like me. (1) *If they can relay all their bitter details, I can share mine.* She took a deep breath and began her story.

Chapter 4

"I do know when and where it happened. As many problems as I have with my memory, this is something I will never forget. I was bitten several years ago, and it wasn't outside in the yard, or at a camp, or on a hike, like most people think of with tick bites. It was actually at my desk in an office building in downtown Brentwood Heights. Before I started modeling, I worked as a receptionist at an employment agency, and that's where it took place."

"Yes, that's one of the many misconceptions about Lyme disease, Julie." The doctor broke in with a sympathetic tone. "It **was** first diagnosed in the New England region, and it **is** more prevalent in the Northeast area of the United States. It does typically happen outdoors. However, many people, even medical professionals, have naively believed that's the **only** places where it exists. But we live in a society that is highly mobile, indoors and out, more so than ever before. Ticks get on animals, people, clothing, vehicles, luggage, anything! They travel just as much as we do, and they bring the disease with them wherever they go, worldwide." (1)

"Exactly!" The model agreed.

"Fortunately, as more research is done, much more is being learned about the disease, and the coinfections that often accompany it, so the tide is slowly turning."

"That's encouraging," she said, then resumed her story. "One day at work, I was wearing a skirt and sandals, so my legs were bare. Suddenly it felt like something had bitten or stung me on my left leg, a little above my ankle." She stopped talking to show the doctor the small round scar that remained at the original site of the bite.

Pulling her socks in place to cover it, she continued. "Almost immediately, the site both itched and hurt. Then I developed a red circular rash, which is typical for some, but not all, tick bites. Of course, I didn't know that then. My boss thought it was a spider bite and sent me to an Urgent Care."

"As you said, Doctor, there's a shocking lack of knowledge about Lyme disease, even in the medical community. There was even less education then than there is now. The doctor who examined me at the clinic that day actually said to me, 'I don't know **what** that is, so I'll just treat you for a spider bite'."

"He gave me a one-week course of a mild oral antibiotic and medications for the pain and itching. I was extremely sick for eight or ten days, with symptoms like a bad case of the flu. My employer was great about the whole thing and even paid me Workers Compensation for the days of work I missed and covered the expenses for my exam and medicines."

"That was a very understanding employer," Doctor Jensen remarked.

"Yes, it was," Julie agreed. "My boss even looked under the desk trying to find whatever bit me, and she couldn't find anything, so they had plausible deniability, but they were good to me when they didn't have to be."

"I'm thankful for that. It was one less thing you had to deal with at the time." Anderson couldn't help but interject his gratitude.

His girlfriend looked at him with a smile. "You're right about that. Anyway, I ultimately recovered and went back to work, and life returned to normal. A short time later I got into modeling, and it proved to be much more physically demanding than the receptionist job had been. As I got more and more active, the routine of being on my feet for hours at a time, traveling, changing time zones… the stress took its toll on me and that's when I started having so many symptoms."

"I would go to the supermarket and forget why I was there, or even how I got there. Then I'd get scared and melt down with an anxiety attack, running from the store in a panic. Frequently I'd have something in mind I wanted to say, but when I opened my mouth, totally different words came out than what I intended. I started having sleep issues, fluctuating back and forth between sleeping a lot and not being able to sleep at all. I felt like I had been drugged much of the time and couldn't think clearly. I've since learned the term for that is 'brain fog', and that describes it very well. Then there was the pain… I got to the point when there were days I literally thought I was going to die from the amount of joint and muscle pain I was in."

"All of this accumulated and I began to get depressed. Everything started affecting my career. Fears escalated that

I would lose my dream that had finally taken off, which seemed to make the symptoms worse. I got stuck in a vicious cycle of fear contributing to the symptoms, and worsening symptoms contributing to the fear."

"When I began to have entire conversations with people that I had no knowledge or recollection of mere moments after they happened, I got even more scared. I didn't understand what was happening to me, and that's when I finally started looking for answers."

Julie had done a great job of staying calm so far, but at this point she had to pause because she was starting to tremble. Anderson stood and began to gently rub her shoulders to help her relax and soon she was able to continue.

"I ended up seeing several different doctors trying to find one who could tell me what was going on. With each new appointment, I would get my hopes up, only to grow progressively more desperate for answers."

"I'm so sorry," Doctor Jensen consoled her. "Unfortunately, this happens far too often, and sometimes severely ill patients even end up losing their lives before they get adequate, effective treatment." (2)

"That's tragic!" Julie exclaimed. "That shouldn't happen!"

"I agree," the doctor said. "It's very disturbing to see the inadequate treatments that are so often presented to these patients. Because of so many inferior diagnostic options, many people don't even know for sure if they have the disease or not. Then things get further complicated because Lyme can imitate so many other infections. Consequently, many people end up getting the wrong diagnosis and poor treatment." (2)

"Yes! That's exactly what happened to me!" the model declared. "I was told by each doctor that something different was responsible for my misery. I was diagnosed with everything from Chronic Fatigue Syndrome to Multiple Sclerosis. One doctor told me it was all in my head and diagnosed me with Clinical Depression, so I started seeing a therapist and taking antidepressants. That helped me cope, but I still was no closer to finding out what was actually wrong with me."

"The last doctor I saw said I had Fibromyalgia. He looked me in the eye and said, 'Since there's no cure, you just have to learn to live with it'. That was one provider I had previously seen a few times and liked, but I lost all respect for him that day and never went back. That's when I gave up on ever solving the mystery."

After recalling the fear, desperation, and hopelessness she felt during those times, a tear slipped from her eye. Anderson gently wiped it away and gave her a reassuring squeeze on her arm. She looked at him with a smile and continued.

"Then I met **this** guy." She indicated her boyfriend and the three of them chuckled. "He was fighting his own health battles and introduced me to Doctor Michaels. I told him I couldn't bear to see one more doctor who would tell me I was crazy. He assured me this one would be different and kept encouraging me to make an appointment with him. Last February I finally did and related everything to him. Wow, it's been over a year since then."

She sniffled a couple of times and grabbed a tissue from the desk nearby. "Sorry for being so emotional about all of this," she offered.

"It's quite alright, Julie," Doctor Jensen responded. "It's an incredibly difficult journey you're on, and it's perfectly understandable for you to be deeply affected by it. Continue when you're ready."

"Thank you for being so patient," she smiled. "Anyway, imagine my surprise when the first thing Doctor Michaels asked was if anyone had ever tested me for Lyme disease. I told him no, not **one** physician I had seen had even mentioned Lyme as a possibility. He immediately had me tested, and the results were positive. He put me on a course of oral antibiotics, but it has only helped minimally. I have continued having significant symptoms, so that's why he sent me to you."

Doctor Jensen sighed. "You have really been through the wringer, and I am so sorry that you've suffered with this. Let me ask you something. What was the approximate time frame between the day you were bitten and when you started having these symptoms?"

Thinking for a moment, Julie replied, "It was about ten years."

"Did you have **any** of the symptoms during that ten-year period?"

"Not that I recall," she said, tearing up again in her frustration. "That's one of the most baffling things about all of this, Doctor. I was **fine**... until I **wasn't**."

Chapter 5

"Those are some of our finest roses this season." The salesperson's voice coming from over her shoulder was unexpected, but Meagan had to agree with the sentiment.

"Oh, yes, they're beautiful! The lovely shades of red, pink, and white are just what I was looking for! They're perfect." Meagan continued gazing at the various sizes, from new buds to fully opened blooms and every size in between.

The helpful clerk replied, "It's great to hear you found a selection you love! May I help you make an arrangement with some of them? What kind of event are you needing them for?"

The older woman smiled at the girl and revealed, "I need a special centerpiece for the table at our family's Valentine dinner. We have been through a great deal the past few years, but things are looking up, so I'm ready to celebrate!"

"That's wonderful!" The salesgirl seemed genuinely happy. "We are glad to be able to help you make the occasion even more grand!"

"Now that we have the perfect flowers, I am hoping to find something equally beautiful to arrange them in. Do you have anything here that you would recommend?"

"We sure do! Follow me, we have a lovely selection available right over here near the cutting tables."

The two crossed the room to the indicated area and Meagan instantly saw an ideal vase. It was tall and oblong, made of frosted pink glass. "Oh my! This is the one! May I please have an arrangement made in this vase, with a mixture of the red, pink and white blooms, varying sizes, with a little fern and baby's breath mingled in?"

With a grin, the clerk answered, "That is a specific and gorgeous-sounding request. I do appreciate a customer who has a vision and knows what she wants!" Grabbing her notepad to jot down the details, she repeated everything back to Meagan to confirm the details.

Next the young lady asked for the name and delivery address and said the display could be dropped off the day before her event if that was convenient. Thanking the girl for her help, she agreed to delivery on the thirteenth and provided the needed information. Cheerfully paying for her order, she left the flower shop.

Next on Meagan's to-do list was a stop at the hospital. *I wonder why Anderson wanted to see me. It seemed important in his text, so I can't wait to find out what's going on.* She pulled into the busy parking lot, absently hoping that this visit wasn't to give her some sort of bad news about Andrew's progress. *Ah, here's an empty spot near the front entrance! I'm having all kinds of good luck today! Maybe that's an encouraging sign.*

~~~

She approached the check-in desk and smiled at the receptionist there. "I don't have an appointment, but if you would, please let Ander… I mean, Doctor Blair, know that Meagan Peters is here. He asked me to stop by today."

"Certainly, Mrs. Peters. He told me he was expecting you. Have a seat and I'll see if he's ready for you." The assistant disappeared into the back area briefly, then came to the lobby and invited Meagan to follow her to the doctor's personal office.

Anderson was there waiting for her and stood to greet her warmly. "Meagan, hello! It's so nice to see you. Thank you so much for coming by. Please, have a seat."

She made herself comfortable in one of the chairs across from the large desk, and he settled into the other one next to her. With a smile, she asked, "Okay, you have me here. Now tell me, what's all this secrecy about? Is something wrong with my husband?"

"Ah, yes, I suppose I have been a bit cryptic, but believe me, I have a very good reason!" The doctor was still being mysterious. "And no, it has nothing to do with Andrew. I assure you, he continues to make progress with his therapy and is doing very well."

Meagan was relieved by the good report, but she was also becoming slightly impatient to know what this visit was all about. "I'm sure you do have a good reason, Doctor Blair," she prompted.

"Oh, please, you don't have to be so formal just because we're in my office!"

Adjusting her position in the seat, she started again with a reserved smile. "Okay, **Anderson**, please, just tell me. What's going on?"

He stood and went around to the other side of his desk. Glancing over at his guest, he pulled a small box from one of the drawers. With a flourish, he handed it to Meagan and returned to his chair with a huge grin on his face.

She looked at him with curiosity and he excitedly motioned for her to open the box. She did as he asked and inside was a stunningly beautiful engagement ring. *What in the world? Now I'm **really** confused!* "Um, this is… lovely, Anderson, but… I… we… you and I…"

Suddenly realizing what she must be thinking, Anderson burst into exuberant laughter. "Oh, Meagan, you should see the look on your face right now! Oh my gosh, I'm so sorry. Let me make myself clear. This ring is a surprise for **Julie**!"

Her entire demeanor changed, and her face lit up as she joined in the merriment. "Oh! Oh, my goodness! Of course, it's for Julie! This is so exciting! We will have another wedding in our little family! This is wonderful news!"

After the initial excitement wore off, she became puzzled again. "Wait a minute. I still don't understand why you asked me here. I mean, I do appreciate you letting me in on the surprise, I just don't know why you would. Besides, you could have told me about it over the phone."

"What, and miss that priceless expression of yours when you saw the ring?" He couldn't help but laugh again just thinking about it.

"Well, what was I supposed to think?" Meagan clearly didn't share Anderson's sense of amusement, so he directed his attention back to her last question.

"Okay, enough about that. I apologize for teasing you. Allow me to explain why I had you come here. It's because I need to ask you for a favor, and I thought it would be nice to do that face to face."

"You want a favor after giving me a hard time?" Meagan looked sternly at him and he was getting worried. Suddenly she started laughing herself. "See there? I can be funny, too!"

"Meagan, you are such a delight!" he declared.

"You should have seen the look on **your** face this time!" The two of them shared another chuckle, then Meagan recovered and prompted, "This must be an important favor you need."

"It is. With Julie's parents overseas, I have been thinking about how to make this proposal really special for her. I know she misses Ron and Cathy very much, and I wish they could be here to participate in this."

If you only knew how desperately Julie needs all the support she can get right now. Of course, it's not my place to go into that. Anderson got a little choked up as he continued.

"I had a video call with them last week and they're extremely excited! Fortunately, I have been given their blessing to propose. I started thinking about how, where, and when to do it, and then I had a great idea! With Valentine's Day right around the corner, and the special dinner you're planning, I was hoping..."

"Yes! Absolutely, yes! It will be perfect for you to propose at the dinner! We have always thought of Julie as family, and now you're going to be part of us too! I mean, even more than you already are!" Meagan quickly hugged Anderson, then took a step back and regained her composure.

Laughing cheerfully, Anderson replied, "I was really hoping you would say that. I didn't want to presume to make this grand gesture without letting you in on it first, so **that** is why I asked you here today. Your parties are always so festive, and I know you go to a lot of trouble to make them memorable. I wouldn't want you to feel like I was trying to steal your thunder."

Meagan clapped her hands together in delight. "You won't be stealing anything! You'll be helping make this one of our most memorable family occasions ever!"

Chapter 6

Julie added some lavender-scented bubble bath to the hot running water. After the day she had, she was looking forward to this. As hard as it was for her to safely maneuver her aching body in and out of the tub, she didn't often indulge in baths these days, but she felt the need for a relaxing soak tonight before bed.

Anderson had insisted on taking her out to eat after the visit with Doctor Jensen, but she wasn't particularly good company. Fortunately, she had a remarkably understanding boyfriend. When she told him before their order was even taken that she really just wanted some time alone to unwind, he agreed to cut their date short and took her home. Of course, he was concerned about her, but he knew they both needed a chance to process all the information they had been given.

Maybe I should at least call Emily. She left me that voicemail hours ago. She's probably worried about me. But I just can't deal with being sociable. Not right now.

Carefully sinking down into the soothing bubbles, Julie closed her eyes and tried to shut out the world. She wanted that more than anything at this point. Instead, she found herself replaying her office visit with Doctor Jensen in her mind.

*I guess I may be obsessing a little bit about all of this, but he gave me **so** much new information! It's a lot to deal with. While I did get many of the answers I've been looking for, it's still incredibly overwhelming.*

She was grateful for the handy design of her bathroom. There was a large area around the tub that allowed her enough space to decorate with a fresh plant and some candles, which she lit now to add some ambiance. There was still room left over for the refreshing glass of iced tea and folder of educational materials she had brought in with her. Doctor Jensen had gathered information from several sources and put it all together in this collection for her to make it easier to review.

With a long swig of the cool beverage, Julie leaned back against her luxurious bath pillow and breathed in the floral scent filling the room. Returning the glass to the space beside the candles, she opened the first pamphlet from the file and began to read.

> Lyme disease is a bacterial illness that can cause fever, fatigue, joint pain, and skin rash, as well as more serious joint and nervous system complications. Lyme disease is the most common vector-borne disease (a disease transmitted by mosquitoes, ticks, or fleas) in the United States. In recent years, approximately 20,000–30,000 confirmed cases of Lyme disease **per year** have been reported to the CDC (Centers for Disease

Control and Prevention). However, the actual number of cases is likely greater than what is reported to health officials. (1)

Although people may think of Lyme as an East Coast disease, it is found throughout the United States, as well as in more than sixty other countries. (2)

The Lyme disease bacterium, *Borrelia burgdorferi*, is spread through the bite of infected ticks. The blacklegged tick (or deer tick, *Ixodes scapularis*) spreads the disease in the northeastern, mid-Atlantic, and north-central United States. The western blacklegged tick (*Ixodes pacificus*) spreads the disease on the Pacific Coast. (3)

Hmm, it's just like Doctor Jensen and I were saying. This sickness really can be anywhere. Why don't people understand that? It doesn't take a genius to grasp the concept. After another drink of her tea, Julie continued.

We have a divided system of medicine and doctors throughout the world: those that are trained to treat causes of chronic disease and those who focus only on medication-based symptomatic care. In all fairness, many doctors don't have the freedom to treat their patients as they would like because medical boards and federal organizations apply political and financial pressure. The reality is sometimes hard to hear but ask those that have been in the middle of this debate and they tell you it gets pretty ugly. There are so many doctors who have differing opinions than the CDC, as well as much more clinical experience than CDC and so-called experts in treating these diseases. So after a patient has been told they're crazy, sent around to various specialists, and is given one of many misdiagnoses, finally the well-trained Lyme literate doctor can run in-depth testing for all infections, co-infections, immune dysfunctions, chemicals, heavy metals, nutritional deficiencies and gather a detailed patient history. And when corrected, their life is vastly improved. (4)

I could definitely go for my life being vastly improved. This describes exactly what happened to me, too! I was told I was crazy, saw multiple doctors, was often misdiagnosed. Apparently, this is the **norm***? This makes me* **really angry***!* Her pulse quickened as her frustration escalated.

Lyme disease is caused by spirochetes, which are coiled bacteria that twist and move, making them difficult to catch and treat in the body. Spirochetes are savvy. They spiral away from antibiotics, burrowing into bones, cells, joints, and nerves. They can even cross the blood-brain barrier, bringing Lyme disease into the central nervous system.

They replicate and spread; all it takes is one dormant spirochete to start reproducing for a Lyme infection to flare up. This is why late-stage Lyme—which goes untreated for a long time and has spread around the body and into the central nervous system—is difficult to treat, if not virtually impossible to fully eradicate. (5)

If Lyme disease is not diagnosed and treated early, the spirochetes can spread and may go into hiding in different parts of the body. Weeks, months or even years later, patients may develop problems with the brain and nervous system, muscles and joints, heart and circulation, digestion, reproductive system, and skin. Different symptoms may appear at different times. (6)

*This is crazy! No wonder it's so controversial. People probably don't want to believe it! This material reads like something out of a science fiction movie. If I had not lived it for myself, **I** wouldn't believe these things were true! But they **are**.*

Chronic Lyme disease occurs when a person who's been treated with antibiotic therapy for the disease continues to experience symptoms. Most people's symptoms improve after six months to a year. It's not known why some people develop post-treatment Lyme Disease Syndrome and others don't. (7)

Julie's bath water was growing cold and the all-too-familiar pain was settling in her joints. *All of this is too much. It's blowing my mind. How is it possible that there can be **so much** information available about this horrible disease, yet **so little** is generally known about it at the same time? I need a break from these brochures. I can't handle any more of this right now.*

Carefully reaching over the side of the tub, she set her glass on a low bench nearby and blew out the candles. She laid the folder containing the baffling information on the bench as well and climbed out of the tub, being very careful not to slip and fall.

Once safely on the plush bathmat, she dried off with a large soft towel, then wrapped herself in her favorite cozy robe. Julie was reaching out for a sense of comfort wherever she could, but the downy fabrics she had surrounded herself with only helped a little.

A gurgling sound from the tub distracted her and she idly turned to see the bubbles disappearing. Bending over to rinse them out the rest of the way, she discovered quickly that she couldn't stay stooped over in that position because it hurt her back. Standing up, she pulled the robe closer and watched the water swirl down the drain. She silently prayed that her newfound hope from this morning wasn't going down with it.

Chapter 7

Julie tossed the offending folder of mind-boggling information onto her queen-size sleigh bed and pulled the fluffy robe a little tighter around her. To assist with the mental breather she needed, she went into the kitchen and decided hot tea would better suit her mood than the cold version she opted for earlier.

She stood by the stove staring absently at the floor as she waited for the water to boil. When the kettle began to whistle loudly a few minutes later, it startled her, and she jumped abruptly. She realized she had once again "checked out", as she called it. Intellectually she knew it had only been for a short time, but every time it happened, it scared her to think that a fugue state **could** last a lot longer.

What if that happened sometime while I was driving? Why does my mind just go blank like that, with no memory of what I was doing during that time? It doesn't happen often, thankfully, but when it does, it totally freaks me out.

Her quest for more information was revived by the stupor, so Julie took the hot tea to her room and settled under the covers in the comfortable bed. She blew on the steaming beverage to help cool it off, then thought better of trying to drink it yet. She sat the mug down on the nightstand and, with a deep breath, picked up the folder again. Looking through the file, she sat aside the documents she read earlier and sorted through the three that remained. Choosing one, she continued reading where she had left off.

> For months and years, mysterious health issues can begin cropping up, becoming more serious over time. These include achy joints, foggy thinking, depression, and shaky hands, to name a few. In an effort to pinpoint a diagnosis, doctors often test for a slew of conditions - lupus, sickle cell disease, fibromyalgia, chronic fatigue syndrome and Lyme. Many people don't notice early signs of Lyme disease, or their medical providers miss the symptoms, which often include fever, headache, fatigue, and a bull's-eye skin rash called erythema migrans, considered the hallmark of the disease. It appears in about 70 to 80 percent of infected people, according to the U.S. Centers for Disease Control and Prevention, although some doctors believe many more cases lack this obvious sign. If Lyme is caught early, it can be treated with antibiotics. But if it goes untreated, the infection can spread to the joints, the heart, and the nervous system. Patients may suffer with severe headaches and neck aches, heart palpitations, facial palsy, and arthritis with severe joint pain. Neurological and memory

problems are often mistakenly blamed on Alzheimer's. (1)

Soon after times of stress (such as moving, getting married or divorced, starting, or losing a job, etc.) symptoms can become profound. A first Lyme blood test may come back negative for Lyme disease, due to the inaccuracy of some lab methods for detecting Lyme. If a patient or their doctor still suspect Lyme, they must insist on further testing. (1)

Doctor Jensen explained this to me in his office, but I was so nervous, it didn't sink in. So, this is why I went for ten years without any of these symptoms. They were lying dormant, hiding, and I didn't even know it. Then I got hit hard when my new modeling schedule ramped up. The sudden increased level of stress was all it took to trigger those nasty little spirochetes to wake up and do their worst. So, the very thing that escalated this, my career, could be the price I pay for having this cursed disease. Unbelievable! Well, this doesn't do anything to change my situation, but at least now I understand it better.

When symptoms do eventually develop, they can be severe, and patients often need aggressive treatment. Intravenous treatment is often required to treat late-stage infection. Late-stage treatment can last many months as seen in other infections as well. Powerful antibiotics through an I.V. for months are sometimes needed to rid the body of the

Lyme disease bacteria. Delayed diagnosis can take a mental and physical toll on the patient. Sometimes a combination of traditional and non-traditional medications may be required, along with changing diet, having blood work done periodically, and not staying on any one drug for long periods of time. The impact that medication has on the body is tremendous. (2)

*Treatment for many months? Seriously? I need to get back to work! How am I supposed to do this for **months**? Don't panic, Julie. Calm down. There's one more pamphlet left. Read that one before you completely lose your mind. Maybe there's hope you don't know about yet.*

A regimen of oral antibiotics is the first course of action against Lyme and many doctors believe the disease just disappears after that but that's not always the case. Often, the bacteria can hide in the body, lingering for months or years and coming back with a vengeance, attacking the central nervous system and brain. Coupled with the fact that a tick bite (what usually transfers Lyme disease) also spreads an average of four other pathogens, the most dangerous of which is Babesia, it's important that when we think of Lyme disease we don't underestimate the coinfections involved. We must take in the full immune-compromised state most patients suffer with. Babesia causes babesiosis, which gives patients malaria-like symptoms, making malaria another common misdiagnosis for the disease. This type of infection can be fatal in one out of ten patients, with an especially increased risk of death in the elderly, the immunosuppressed and those coinfected with Lyme disease. (3)

Co-infections? **Fatal** *in ten percent of patients? How is it possible that the bite of one tiny little tick can do* **so** *much damage? Why isn't more being done to prevent the spread of this despicable disease?*

Checking the mug on the nightstand and finding the tea had cooled enough not to burn her, she closed her eyes and savored a few long sips. She desperately wished it had the power to wash away all her concerns, but of course, no tea could do that.

Looking around her bed at the brochures scattered across the comforter, she couldn't help but think of the irony. *Why is it called a comforter? It's a blanket! It can't comfort me any more than this tea can. Neither of them can help me at all!*

Julie shuddered at the thought. Her mind was spinning from all the information she had read. She felt angry, frustrated, and overwhelmed. The combination of emotions was too much, and she began to cry. The tears became heavy sobs that wracked her body, and she hurled the mug across the room. As it shattered against the wall, tea dripping down onto the floor, she tried to come to terms with the vast amount of data that had been presented to her today, and what it all meant.

So, this is where we are. The oral medications Doctor Michaels treated me with weren't effective, so Doctor Jensen will be setting me up for the insertion of the PICC (peripherally inserted central catheter) *line and we'll go that route. I'll have an IV going from my left arm to a vein that carries blood to my heart, and the antibiotics will go through that tube. I'll be a science experiment for **months**!*

***Why** did this happen to me? Why does it happen to **anyone**? It's just not right! In this day and age, with all the medical and technological advances available, how can this horrible illness **still** be so **grossly** misunderstood?*

For lack of any other way to release her rage, she swiped into the floor the folder and all the brochures of grim information that both terrified and infuriated her. She didn't care that it made a mess, she just couldn't bear to look at it.

Next, she grabbed a pillow and squeezed it tightly, then screamed into it as loudly as she could several times. When that still wasn't enough to relieve her emotions, she punched it over and over again. Finally, she kicked the bed like a spoiled toddler, and continued the outburst until she exhausted herself and lacked the energy to continue.

Eventually she calmed down and started thinking more rationally. That was the night that Julie Chambers made a solemn vow. *If I survive this beast, I'm going to use every avenue available to me to educate people about it and try to help win the war against Lyme disease!*

Chapter 8

Anderson was a nervous wreck. It was finally Valentine's Day, the dinner he had been waiting for was tonight, and he had been excitedly looking forward to proposing to Julie, so why was he feeling so nervous and jumpy? He nearly called one of his patients the wrong name yesterday and then cut himself shaving this morning, both of which almost never happen.

He was standing in his walk-in closet trying to choose what to wear for this momentous occasion, which was proving to be no easy decision. *How do I dress to look exactly right for a beautiful girl who is a fashion model? What am I doing dating a model in the first place? What's wrong with me, even thinking about asking someone like her to marry me? Have I lost my mind?*

His phone rang somewhere in the distance, bringing him out of his reverie. *Where did I leave my phone? The insistent buzzing continued. I know it's here somewhere! Obviously, it's here, Anderson, or you wouldn't hear it ringing. Just follow the sound, nitwit.* Buzz. Buzz.

Tossing pillows off the couch into the floor, his search became more frantic. If he weren't a doctor concerned about a possible emergency, he would just give up. Buzz. Buzz.

*That's right, I'm not a nitwit. I'm a **doctor**, for Pete's sake! A doctor who can't find his blasted phone.*

He got closer to the coat rack by the front door and realized the sound was growing louder. He found the device in his coat pocket and answered it just in time to hear the dial tone. *Of course. It took me so long to find it, the call finally went to voicemail.* Checking the last number on the screen, he saw that the missed call was from Meagan.

Before he could call her back, the phone beeped in his hand, signaling he had a new text. Opening the message, he saw it was from Meagan, too.

[Anderson, where are you? This is a very important day and you're late!]

Well, now I'm even later, Meagan, because I had to drop what I was doing to find my phone! More frustrated than ever, he rushed back to figure out what to wear.

~~~

Julie looked at herself in the full-length mirror in the powder room at the Peters' house. She had arrived early to help Meagan get things ready. It had been awhile since she spent any one-on-one time with the woman who was like a second mother to her, so she wanted to volunteer her assistance and get that precious time.

Gazing at her reflection, she liked what she saw for the first time in a while. *I've been looking so pale and tired, and now I look more like myself. I don't know **why**, since I haven't started treatment with Doctor Jensen yet. Maybe it's just the fact that I finally have answers and a plan. Stressful as the prospect of all that is, there is some measure of peace in knowing.*

44

She smoothed her blonde hair, the curls falling elegantly over her shoulders, and adjusted the hem of the red dress she wore. The white pearls, a gift from her mother on her 18th birthday, completed the classic look. Satisfied, she turned off the light and returned to the kitchen to see what else she could do to help with dinner.

"I don't know **where** your boyfriend is," Meagan announced randomly, bustling around the room like a skittish cat. "He should have been here by now."

That's strange. Why is she so concerned about when Anderson gets here? Nobody else has arrived yet either and it's still early. "Don't worry, I'm sure he will be here soon. Why does it even mat… Oh! Meagan! Look! That pot is boiling over!" Both women rushed toward the stove at the same time and slammed right into each other.

The dish of diced tomatoes Meagan was carrying landed smack between them on impact, spilling the contents all down the front of Julie's beautiful dress. "Oh! My dear, I'm so sorry! Your dress!" Meagan was mortified.

"Forget the dress, the water in the pot is spilling all over the stove!" In her efforts to rescue the saucepan, Julie didn't notice that hot fluid had already reached the floor. In one fell swoop, her foot found the puddle and down she went.

The older woman had enough wits about her to quickly turn off the heat on the stove and move the overflowing mess into the sink. Returning her attention to her pseudo daughter, she found the young lady in a disheveled heap on the floor. Her blonde hair was obscuring her face, but it was evident her body was shaking.

Expecting to find Julie in tears, Meagan knelt beside her and spoke softly. "Come on, now, Dear, it's not as bad as all that. Here, let me help you stand up. Are you alright? Are you hurt? Did the water burn you?"

Suddenly Julie tossed her head back, revealing the cause for her trembling. She wasn't crying, rather she was giggling so intensely, the power of speech was difficult. Finally, she managed, "Oh, my goodness! If anyone could have seen us… that whole incident must have looked like a scene with a couple of comedians from a TV show!"

Before she knew it, Meagan lost her footing and plopped down on the floor as well. She couldn't help but join in the hilarity, and soon the two of them had tears rolling down their cheeks and their sides ached from laughing so hard.

~~~

When he walked into the kitchen a few minutes later, Anderson stopped in his tracks and stared. Expecting to find his hostess annoyed by his tardiness, he was surprised by the site that greeted his arrival instead.

There was the always dignified Meagan Peters, on the floor in front of the stove, her lovely pink dinner dress wrinkled, one high heel on and one off. Beside her was his beloved Julie, the woman he had been so concerned about impressing tonight with his appearance. She too was in complete disarray, her elegant red dress covered in… what was that? Tomatoes? The strangest part was they both were laughing hysterically.

"So, this is what happens when I'm running late? I miss all the fun?" Anderson teased. The women looked at each other and burst into a whole new round of hilarity.

Checking out the rest of the kitchen made him even more curious. "What is going on with you two? This place

46

looks like it was hit by a tornado, and you gals are a **mess**! Is there something I can do to help?"

Again, the only response was uncontrolled giggling. At that moment, Andrew, Nick, and Emily joined the party, and found themselves as baffled as Anderson was.

"What's happening here?" Andrew whispered. "Are they alright?"

"I couldn't say," Anderson replied with a shrug. "I've not been able to get a word out of them."

"Maybe we would be safer in the living room!" Nick suggested.

"Maybe we would!" The other two agreed.

"Oh, you guys, let me handle this," Emily offered, shooing the three men away as if they were naughty children.

With final glances over their shoulders and whispers between themselves, the three made their escape before Nick's wife could change her mind and try to enlist their assistance. Once they were a safe distance away, Emily returned her attention to the ladies on the floor.

"Okay, Mom, Julie, I got rid of the guys. Do you think you can bring the levity down a notch or two and let me in on the joke? What's so funny?" Emily was using a tone just stern enough to get the attention of the others.

They managed to pull themselves up from the floor and her mother grumbled, "Well, you're no fun, Emily."

"Mom!" Her daughter was shocked at such a remark from her typically solemn parent.

"Oh, she's just kidding, Em," Julie defended. "It was a comedy of errors that got the better of us and we just... well, we just lost it!"

Emily began wiping up pieces of tomatoes off the floor. "You can tell me all about it while the three of us clean up this kitchen. Then we better get some dinner on the table, or we're going to have three hangry men to deal with. We don't want that, because then nobody will be laughing!"

Chapter 9

The men had made their escape and were relaxing in the living room. They could hear the ladies in the kitchen, but they were wisely staying at a safe distance. Nick stoked the logs on the fire then joined his father-in-law on the couch.

"So, you have no idea what that was all about?" he asked Anderson, grinning.

"They were like that when I got here," he shrugged, chuckling a bit himself.

"I asked what was going on, but they couldn't stop laughing long enough to tell me!"

"I don't think I've ever seen my dear wife in such a state!" Andrew snickered. "Even when we met in college, she was so refined, and has remained so. I have to say, it did my heart good to see her cut loose like that!"

Anderson absently patted the small box in his pocket. *This evening sure hasn't started out anything like I expected! My plan was to get here early and take Julie aside and make the proposal quiet and intimate. Now, after seeing her happier than I ever have, and being reminded of the warmth and love in this family, I think I have a better idea.*

~~~

"Come and get it, boys!" Emily's called out cheerfully.

Nick led the way to the dining room and wrapped his arms around his wife's waist. "Are you sure it's safe for us to enter?"

Playfully pushing him away, she swatted his arm and said, "Enter at your own risk, but if you want to eat this dinner we've worked hard on, I suggest you all sit down and don't argue with us!"

Andrew took his place at the head of the table and reached to the seat beside him, taking Meagan's hand in his. "Sweetheart, everything looks so beautiful tonight. The table, this colorful flower arrangement, the food…" He paused and kissed the back of her hand. "And especially you, My Love. You've never looked more enchanting than you do right now. Happy Valentine's Day."

Misty-eyed with emotion, she returned the kiss and beamed at her husband. "That was wonderful, Andrew. Thank you! I love you, and Happy Valentine's Day to you as well, Darling."

Not to be outdone, at the other end of the table, Nick turned to Emily. "This is quite a different Valentine's Day from last year, but this one is even better. We have **so** many blessings, especially our sweet baby on the way. I love you more today than on our wedding day, and I mean the **first** one!"

Everyone laughed, then Emily gave her husband a quick kiss. "I'm not going to get all sentimental like the rest of you right now or I'll start blubbering in my plate. Blame that on the pregnancy hormones! Just know that I love you with all my heart, Babe. Happy Valentine's Day!"

Anderson took a deep breath. *I was going to wait until after dinner, but now seems like the perfect time. I changed my mind once tonight already, so I guess I can change it again.*

Standing and clearing his throat to get everyone's attention, he decided to dive right in. "While everybody here is so full of love on this special occasion, I have a few things I would like to say, as well. Nick's right, we all have so much to be grateful for. Heck, there was a time when this guy couldn't stand the sight of me, and yet here we are, having dinner together, and not for the first time!"

Chuckles flourished around the table and Nick raised his iced tea glass and cheered, "Here, here!" Everyone else raised their glasses too in a silly toast until Anderson tried to regain control of the conversation.

"Alright, alright, I'm trying to be serious you guys. What is it in the air in this house tonight? Did the pest control company come spray it with laughing gas this afternoon or something?"

That set everyone off again and he had to take the blame for that one. *Okay, that **was** pretty funny. Am I stalling by making jokes because I'm nervous? Pull yourself together, man! Don't blow it!*

Anderson started again. "**Anyway**, I'm trying to say that I'm extremely glad all of you came into my life and that we've become such a tight-knit little group. You have all become very special to me." He turned and smiled warmly at Julie, who was still seated beside him.

"Of course, one of you has become **extremely** special to me. Julie, when we met, I wasn't sure you would give me the time of day, much less agree to go on a date with me.

When you did, I was over the moon, and things get better and better with you every day."

Reaching into his pocket, he pulled out the box and knelt on one knee in front of her. "Oh!" she blurted, bringing her hands to her mouth as it dawned on her what was happening. Emily had the foresight to grab her phone and start recording.

"Julie Paige Chambers, you have changed my life for the better. You are the only woman in this crazy world for me, and I love you with all my heart. So, in front of our dearest friends, with tomato… whatever that is… all down the front of your lovely red dress, will you please do me the honor of becoming my wife?"

Squealing loud enough the neighbors could probably hear, she threw her arms around his neck and exclaimed, "Yes! Yes! Absolutely, yes!" He slid the stunning ring on her finger and kissed her tenderly.

Standing together with their arms around each other, the couple was beaming. "Okay, Nick, **now** you can make a toast!"

~~~

After congratulations and hugs all around, everyone settled back down in their seats and finally filled their plates with the delicious food the ladies had prepared. Between bites of fresh green salads, warm crescent rolls, and savory chicken cacciatore, the women finally explained the series of events that happened earlier which landed them on the floor in fits of laughter. The guys had to admit it sounded hilarious, and everyone was quite amused by the story.

Julie had never been happier. She was completely surprised by Anderson's proposal, and kept looking at her left hand to be sure it was real. Every so often he would notice her out of the corner of his eye and would turn and smile at her. She would pretend to be embarrassed that he caught her gazing at the striking ring, but he knew her joy was real.

It was a simple piece of jewelry, since the physical therapist was just starting to get back on his feet and pay off some of his medical bills. He felt it was perfect for his bride-to-be though, as it was elegant and classic, just like her. The band was white gold with two baguette diamonds, one on each side of the princess cut solitaire in the center. It was exactly what he would have chosen for her if he had all the money in the world to spend.

"When do you two lovebirds think you might like to have the wedding?" Meagan asked eagerly.

"Mom! Give them time. They just got engaged less than an hour ago!" Emily scolded. "I know you mean well, but let's not be pushy!"

"It's okay, Emily. We appreciate your interest, Mom," Julie smiled. "I need to talk to my parents first. This will be a big surprise, and of course, I want them to be part of the ceremony."

Anderson spoke up with a grin. "Do you think I would have the audacity to propose to you without getting your parents' permission first? What kind of man do you think I am?"

The group around the table got quiet as the bride-to-be took in what her fiancé was saying. "You mean… you talked to my parents… and they know? That's amazing, Babe! When?"

"Of course I did! I had a very nice video chat with Ron and Cathy last week. They were thrilled and gave me their unconditional blessing!"

Delighted once again, Julie continued, "Well, aren't you just full of surprises?

You always manage to amaze me."

"Good to know," he teased. "Amazing you is what I live for."

Chapter 10

"Okay, then," Julie suggested. "I don't know about you, Honey, but I would love to get married in…"

"The Fall!" the couple exclaimed together, and everyone cheered.

"Yes!" Julie declared. "We both have always said Fall is our favorite time of year, and it would give us several months to arrange everything."

The others eagerly voiced their agreement.

"That sounds great!"

"It's perfect!"

"Fall weddings are always so pretty."

Anderson stood once more and Nick joked, "Hey, man, what are you doing now? Are you going to propose **again**?"

"No, smart guy, I just have something else I want to say." Resuming a more serious tone, he again directed his comments to Julie. "It's true that we do share a love of the Fall season, but there's another reason I would like to marry you then. Honey, given all that you've been through, I can honestly say you are the strongest woman I know. While there are many reasons I love you, that's one of the main ones."

"Thank you for saying that, Babe," she replied. "Sometimes I don't feel very strong, but I'm really touched to hear that you see me that way."

"I definitely do," he asserted. "So, they say red leaves fall off the trees last because they are the strongest, and that strength keeps them holding on. They don't like to give up. (1) I see that trait in you. You're my red leaf girl! That being said, the red leaves on the trees in the Fall seem like the perfect backdrop for our wedding."

Deeply touched by his words, even more than the rest of the party knew, Julie stood and wrapped her hand in his. With an emotional catch in her voice, she looked around the table and said, "How romantic is this guy? Okay, it's settled. We will be getting married this Fall! Actual date to be determined. Happy Valentine's Day, everybody!"

~~~

After dinner, the group lingered over cups of hot chocolate, chatting about the wedding and other, less exciting subjects. They just didn't want to part ways quite yet, and there was a spirit of warmth that had settled over everyone. Well, almost everyone.

Julie had excused herself to go to the powder room, and when she opened the door to leave, she was quickly pushed back inside by Emily's insistent shove.

Startled by her friend's behavior, she tried to protest, but was quickly cut off.

"Okay, Missy, everyone else may not have been paying attention, but I was, so out with it!" One more nudge made Julie plop town on the stool beside the sink.

Looking up at Emily towering over her, she felt like an errant student being reprimanded by an angry teacher. "What in the world are you talking about?"

"You know exactly what I'm talking about!"

"No, I really don't."

Emily composed herself and started again, more calmly this time. "What was all that stuff Anderson was saying about red leaves and you being so strong after all you've been through?"

Julie could feel her cheeks flush with unease and that feeling of an errant student deepened. "Oh… that…" she gulped. *What do I say?*

"Yes, **that**." Emily looked defiant and more than a little hurt as she crossed her arms and waited for an explanation.

"Em, this **really** isn't the time or the place…"

"When **is** the time and place? You have been avoiding me for weeks! You don't return my calls. **What** is going on with you, Jules? I'm supposed to be your best friend, so why won't you talk to me?"

The blonde stood and wrapped the redhead in her arms as they both started to cry. "Emily, you **are** my best friend! I've been wanting to talk to you about this for months, but every time I try, something happens, and it's never been the right time."

"So, I'm not imagining things. There really is something going on that I don't know about. I told Nick I wasn't crazy."

Trying to defuse the situation with humor, Julie pulled out of the hug and said, "Well, the jury's still out on **that**!"

Her friend was not amused. "Very funny," she quipped sarcastically. "So, when can we talk, and it better be **soon**!"

I'm having the surgery to put in my PICC line in a couple of weeks, so she's right, I can't put it off any longer. We have to finally have this conversation.

"How about lunch tomorrow?" Julie suggested. "Is that soon enough?"

"Yes!" Emily squealed. "That will work!"

The two walked arm-in-arm back to the living room to join the rest of the group. "It's about time," Nick taunted playfully. "We were ready to send in a search and rescue team!"

Andrew asked if everyone was up for a few hands of cards. Four of them were, but there was one couple who sheepishly begged off. They did just get engaged, after all. Saying their goodbyes, Anderson and Julie left for the evening. As they walked out, they remembered they had arrived separately, so they agreed to meet at her apartment, and he followed her home.

~~~

Rushing inside, Julie hurriedly lit a few candles and dimmed the lights. The glow sparkled off the diamond on her finger and when he walked in, he caught her gazing at it. Again. Taking her in his arms, he kissed her tenderly. "You made me the happiest man in the world tonight, Julie Chambers."

She returned his kiss then replied, "You made me the happiest girl, Anderson Blair." She laid her head on his shoulder and they let the magnitude of the evening sink in.

"Did I really surprise you?" he finally asked, sure he already knew the answer.

"Are you kidding? I've never been more surprised in my life!" Her expression suddenly changed, and she added, "Well, not with a **good** surprise, anyway." She pulled away from him and sat down on the sofa. Kicking off her heels, she started rubbing her aching feet.

Anderson sat beside her and coaxed her to turn and put her legs across his lap. As he began to massage the soreness of one foot, he asked, "What's wrong? Your mood just dropped. You seem upset."

"Emily cornered me tonight as I was coming out of the powder room. She demanded to know what all your talk of strength and red leaves was about."

"Oh no!" he exclaimed. "I was so caught up in the romance of the moment, I just let what was in my heart blurt right out my mouth! I'm so sorry, Babe. I never meant to betray your confidence. What was I thinking? Clearly, I **wasn't** thinking!"

She giggled and responded sweetly, "It's okay, Honey, don't worry about it. I was hoping to talk to Emily tonight anyway. I was going to ask her if we could get together and chat. That's what ended up happening when it was all said and done, so the end result was the same. Don't beat yourself up over it. Tonight was perfect."

"You certainly are an understanding woman." He grinned and went to work on her other foot. "I know it isn't going to be easy for you to rehash all of this **again**. It's not going to be easy for Emily to hear, either. So, when are you gals going to have this long-awaited conversation?"

"We're meeting for lunch tomorrow. There's no time like the present. I've been putting it off long enough." She stretched her arms and wiggled her toes. "My aching feet thank you. That feels so good! I'm starting to realize there are benefits to being **engaged** to a physical therapist!" She held up her left hand with a huge smile, waving it around to watch the light dance off the gems again.

He looked at her lovingly and murmured, "It makes my heart smile to see you so happy. You know what?"

"What?" she asked, still admiring her ring.

"You're going to make some lucky man a great wife one day."

Chapter 11

Emily sat waiting not-so-patiently at the cafe where she and Julie were meeting for lunch. *I **knew** something was up with her! I'm upset she hasn't confided in me before now, but I guess I understand what she meant about timing. There's always **something** going on with this family. Knowing her, she didn't want to take away from anything else or make me worry about her when I've had other things to deal with. She really is amazing and so unselfish. Maybe I need to cut her some slack today. Goodness knows, I gave her a hard enough time last night!*

"You look positively radiant!" Julie complimented her friend as she joined her at the quiet corner table. This was one of their favorite spots, and she was grateful they would have both familiarity and privacy for their talk.

"Thank you! Pregnancy agrees with me!" Emily beamed.

"Yes, I remember from the first…" The blonde stopped mid-sentence but worried it may already be too late. "Oh, Em, I'm so sorry. I shouldn't have…"

Tucking her auburn hair behind one ear, she reached across the table to pat Julie's hand. "It's okay. Since I regained my memories of Sarah Beth, I actually find comfort in thinking about her, and talking about her. I'm grateful I was able to carry her to term, to hold her and see her sweet face, to say goodbye. Remembering the loss and going through that all over again was agonizing, but I've had time to come to grips with it now."

With a genuine smile Julie replied, "That's wonderful. I'm so happy to hear you are in a good place and can enjoy your memories of her."

"I do, and thank you for saying that."

"That dress looks so pretty on you! Blue has always been your color!"

"Thanks for that, too, but you're stalling. We aren't here to talk about me."

"I know. I'm sorry. Let's order and then I promise to tell you everything."

The waitress came and soon they had delicious chicken salad wraps and hot tea to enjoy. "So, you know I've not been feeling well for a while…" Julie proceeded to relate the entire painful experience in detail as Emily sat listening in baffled silence. About an hour later, Julie had proudly managed to share her story without crying once.

"My dear, precious friend, this is…" The redhead searched for the right word, finding it difficult to come up with one. She finally abandoned the attempt and just shook her head in distress as she pushed a bite of her wrap around on the plate.

"I know," Julie said. "It's a lot to process. I'm still working on that myself."

Lifting her gaze, Emily groaned, "You went through all of this alone! Why didn't you come to me? I would have been there for you. I would have gone to all those doctors with you!"

"Em, I know you would have, but in the beginning, I kept thinking I would feel better soon. I tried to convince myself that it was no big deal, that I could handle it. By the time my symptoms intensified, you had just had your accident, so there was no way I was going to lay this on you. Then you and Nick were getting married, then everything happened with your dad…"

"Then you met Anderson. **He** has been there for you. That explains his cryptic references to your strength and the red leaves last night. Now it all makes sense."

Looking across the table, Julie inquired, "Are you mad at me? It's not that I didn't want you around. Believe me, I would have welcomed your help! I was just trying not to burden you even more than you already were."

With a resigned sigh Emily replied, "No, of course I'm not mad at you. I just feel bad that I wasn't there for you, that's all. To think of everything you've been through; it's all so overwhelming!"

"Well, you're here for me now," her friend encouraged. "I'm going to need someone to drive me to the hospital in a couple of weeks to have the PICC line outpatient surgery. And I'll need a ride home afterward. Do you suppose you might know anyone who would volunteer?"

"Hmm, let me think," Emily teased, twisting a section of auburn hair around her finger. "I'm pretty sure I can come up with someone."

"See there? I knew I could count on you!" Julie praised.

Raising her teacup for a toast, Emily smiled, "To best friends!"

"I will drink to that!" The model joined in with a hearty, "Cheers!" and they playfully clinked their cups together.

Seeing their waitress approaching with the fresh fruit cups they had ordered to finish off the meal, Emily asked, "Not to downplay the severity of your situation at all, but would it be okay if we change to a lighter subject while we have dessert?"

"Of course, please! I welcome a lighter subject! Which do you prefer we talk about… you being my Matron of Honor or me hosting your baby shower?" Julie popped a fresh strawberry in her mouth and savored the natural sweetness.

"We have the rest of the afternoon, My Dear." Emily enthused, waving her fork in the air and nearly dropping the chunk of pineapple from it. "Let's talk about both!"

~~~

"How was lunch?" Nick asked that night as he and his wife were getting ready for bed. She was sitting on the stool at her vanity brushing her long hair. He had just walked out of the en suite bathroom and stood leaning in the doorway, lost in the joy of watching her.

When we first met, I didn't think she could possibly be any more beautiful. Now, looking back at all we've been through together, I appreciate how it has brought us closer, and that makes her even more attractive to me. Now she's carrying another child, which we never dared hope for. And that hair! Wow…

"It was interesting, to say the least," Emily responded.

"Huh? What was interesting?" The man was clearly distracted.

Turning away from the mirror, she good-naturedly waved the hairbrush at him and scolded, "Nick Peterson, are you standing there ogling me?"

He crossed the room, took the brush from her, and began to tend to her long mane himself. "Am I not allowed to ogle my own gorgeous wife?"

"Of course you are!" she exclaimed.

"Good, because you can't stop me!" he declared.

Giggling, she stood and darted to the bed, quickly getting under the covers. Nick dropped the brush on the floor and hastily joined her, wrapping his arm around her and snuggling close.

"Okay, so, tell me… what was interesting?" He resumed their conversation.

"Aha, so you **were** paying attention!" She nudged him playfully under the covers for emphasis.

"My dear wife, I am deeply offended." He put his hand over his heart and pretended to be insulted. "I pay attention to every scintillating word that comes out of your lovely mouth. To imply anything less is simply…"

Pulling back and looking him in the eye, she gave him the best stern look she could muster. "Really, Nick? Don't you think you're laying it on a **little** heavy?"

Together they burst into laughter, then burrowed back into the comfort of their love nest. "Okay, okay, all joking aside. Don't keep me in suspense any longer. What is going on with Julie?" Nick was genuinely concerned.

"I will tell you, but it's going to be hard to believe." Emily shared as much as she could recall of the details her best friend had given her. As expected, her husband found the information as shocking and upsetting as she had.

"I had no idea Lyme disease was so misunderstood. Heck, it's apparently even controversial. With millions of infected people all over the world, how is that even possible?" He was talking to himself as much as he was to his wife.

Shaking her head, she agreed. "I know. It's bizarre, to say the least. I'm still having trouble processing it."

"It's irresponsible and senseless, that's what it is," Nick acknowledged.

Even in the darkening room, with only the moon to light his face, Emily knew that look in his eye. Subtly encouraging him she suggested, "You're so right, My Love. You know what? Somebody really should do something about it."

The wheels were turning, and she smiled at him, knowing the lightbulb would soon turn on. "Yes, **somebody** should..." he muttered thoughtfully. And there it was.

Chapter 12

"I don't think I can do this," Julie confided. "I've been in panic mode all morning!" It was surgery day and she was rushing around trying to get ready to go, but when her best friend arrived to pick her up, she was mainly going in circles.

Emily blocked the path and held up her hands. "Stop! You **can** do this. You have been thoroughly informed about what to expect, you are well prepared, and, let's face it, you have no choice. It's a done deal. It's happening."

The blonde came to a halt and glared at her, stunned. "Seriously? 'I have no choice?' Is that the best you've got? You're not particularly good at this reassurance thing today, Em."

"I'm sorry, Jules. We're in uncharted waters, here! I thought maybe some tough love would help." Emily shrugged helplessly.

Plopping down on the couch, the model sighed, "You thought wrong." She took a deep breath then finally confessed the truth. "I'm sorry, Emily. I didn't mean to snap at you. I know you're trying to help. It's just that… well… I'm scared."

Her friend sat beside her and held her hand. "That's understandable. But I'll be there with you. You're not alone."

Julie managed a weak smile. "I know. That's not the issue. I just wish they were going to put me to sleep. I could go in, have a nice snooze, wake up, and it would all be over. What's freaking me out is that I'll be **awake**. Doctor Jensen even said I can watch the procedure if I want to. Why in the world would I want to **watch**?"

Emily involuntarily shuddered at the thought. "Sorry, that wasn't helpful, but I couldn't stop it. I agree with you on that; I wouldn't want to watch either. But I **do** know you **can** do this! Remember, you're **strong**! You're red leaves!"

That made both of them chuckle and Julie felt better enough to finish getting ready. As they passed by the console table in her entryway, she grabbed her keys, then picked up a framed photo of Anderson that was displayed there. "Do you think Doctor Jensen would let me take this inside the surgery suite with me? I could look at it during the procedure and have something pleasant to focus on, keep me calm. That would help me tremendously! You don't think they would take it away, do you?"

Considering her friend's words briefly, Emily looked from the picture to Julie's distressed expression. "You know what?" she asked. "I dare that doctor or anyone else to **try**!"

~~~

The redhead paced around the waiting room. *Today there's a patient and an **impatient**! This procedure was supposed to take about two hours and it's already been...* She checked her watch anxiously and sat down with a sigh. *It's only been an hour and a half. I wish Nick was here... or Anderson... or both of them. It's a shame they had to work today. Calm down, Emily. They allowed her to take in the* *photo and stood it up beside her where she could look at it the whole time and not have to witness any of the surgery. I'm sure she is fine… everything is fine. Just* **breathe**.

"Hey, how is she?" Anderson seemed to appear out of nowhere, startling Emily out of her anxious thoughts.

"Do you have to sneak up on me like that?" she snapped, then realized how rude it sounded. "Gosh, I'm sorry. I didn't mean to be so abrupt. I'm just nervous. What are you doing here? I thought you had patients today."

He laughed it off and replied, "I did, and I saw them, but my last one was sick and had to reschedule, so I finished up early. Is she still in surgery?"

"I guess so. I haven't heard anything yet, but it's only been…"

"Mrs. Peterson?" Doctor Jensen's timing couldn't have been better. "Oh, hello Doctor Blair. Glad to see you were able to make it after all."

"How is she?" They both spoke at once.

"She's in recovery now and doing well. You can take her home soon. First, let's go to my office and have a chat."

The two looked at each other, both thoughtfully wondering if something was wrong and why he wanted to talk with them. They followed the doctor silently, but once seated across from him at his desk, Anderson spoke up.

"What's going on? Why do you need to speak with us? Is something wrong?"

"Oh, no, everything went very well. Julie did great! Having that picture of you with her was an inspired idea."

The therapist looked puzzled. "She had a picture of me? Why?"

Emily sheepishly replied, "She was super nervous this morning, so she brought it with her. She said it would help keep her calm to look at it during the procedure."

He grinned. "Well, isn't that sweet? It's kind of like I was there with her."

Doctor Jensen continued. "She's a strong woman, and I am confident that this course of treatment will be successful for her. I brought the two of you in here to see if you have any questions for me about what happens next. Since you are Julie's support system, I want to be sure everyone is clear about this process."

"Thanks for that," Anderson said. "I know you gave Julie instructional papers about how to dispense the medication and take care of the PICC line, but if it wouldn't be too much trouble, would you please review that information with us?"

"Absolutely! That's why I asked you for this visit, so we can go over the details and be sure the two of you know as much as she does, in case she needs your help."

"That sounds wise," Emily concurred. "We want to be prepared to help."

"I'm happy she has such a good support system. Having that foundation is going to be very important. Julie has a long road ahead, and I'll be honest, it's not going to be easy. There will be times she gets discouraged, and there will also be times she wants to quit. I'm counting on you not to let her do that, and to keep her built up."

"Don't worry, Doc, we love that girl more than you can imagine. We'll take excellent care of her." Anderson's face lit up when he talked about his fiancée.

"That's what I'm counting on!" Doctor Jensen declared. "So, let's go over these details, and then our patient should be ready to go home."

The doctor proceeded to explain. "I'll be sending supplies home with Julie that include one carton of IV bags full of antibiotics, another carton with IV bags of saline, and an arm protection sleeve to keep the PICC line from getting wet in the shower. She's not to submerge her left arm in water in any way, including in a hot tub or swimming pool. For the next 24 hours, she needs to apply a warm pack to the PICC line area for 30 minutes, every 2 hours. She needs to take 400 milligrams of ibuprofen three times a day for the next 3 days to help prevent inflammation, soreness, and infection. She should avoid activities that require a lot of movement of the left arm, and no heavy lifting over 5 to 10 pounds." (1)

"She will need to flush the line with saline before the antibiotic, then infuse the entire medication bag, then flush the line again afterward. This helps keep the line clean and open, and also helps prevent clots. (1) The infusion process takes a little while, so she may sit in a chair or lie down while it's going on, as long as she's comfortable and relaxed. She'll need to be sure not to open the port too much, as that would cause the liquid to flow through the line too quickly, which tends to feel very strange and makes many patients dizzy."

"The IV medication will be administered on a pulsing (intermittent) basis which takes advantage of the infections' life cycles. This approach has the additional benefit of allowing the body to recover between treatment cycles." (2)

"The insertion site needs to be monitored for any signs of infection or other complications. Things to look out for are swelling, pain, redness, red streaking, heat or hardness at the site, fever or chills, swelling of her left hand, arm, or the left side of her neck, and leaking of fluid when she flushes the line. If any of those things happen, please contact my office immediately." (1)

"This five-step approach is an individualized program. Those steps are evaluation, stabilization, treatment, healing and, ultimately, remission. Julie will be closely monitored to track her progress and we'll adjust her program accordingly to best meet her goals." (2)

Anderson and Emily looked at each other in silence. Doctor Jensen understood. "This is a great deal of information, and it's going to be a lot for all of you to handle. Life is going to look quite different for a while. It will be worth it all, though, you'll see. I have every confidence in Julie as a patient and in her team of allies!"

Chapter 13

"That's a great idea!" Karen had just heard Nick's plan for the next series he wanted to do on Peterson's Place, and she was totally on board. "I have a friend who went through a very similar experience to Julie's. She went to multiple doctors, was insulted by them and misdiagnosed, just like so many others have had happen to them. It wasn't until she was referred to a Lyme Literate Doctor (LLD) that she was tested and finally got treatment."

"See! That's exactly what I'm talking about!" Nick's exasperation about the issue was evident. "This is happening to patients all over the world, and it's got to **stop**! Hey, do you think your friend would be willing to be a guest on an episode of the show and talk about her experience?"

"Willing, yes. Able, no." Her boss looked puzzled, so Karen explained. "She lives across the country and is in worse condition than Julie is. She isn't mobile enough to make a trip like that to travel here."

Nick got up from his chair and started pacing around the conference room with "that look" on his face. From years of experience as his assistant, Karen knew what that look meant, so she quietly waited. *I love to watch him when he's in the zone. I can almost see the creativity flowing through his mind, like he's giving birth to an idea. I'm not always around to get to witness it, but it's a privilege when I am!*

Her boss snapped his fingers and posed the question, "What if we went to her? Do you think she would do it then?"

His colleague thought about it for a moment, then replied, "I really don't know, Nick, but I can reach out to her and ask. What are you suggesting, exactly?"

"We send a production crew to her, have her join us via a live video feed. It might even make more of an impact than if she was here in person. It would be **real**, showing the effects of this awful disease, how limiting it can be."

"I don't know about that," she hesitated. "I'm not willing to reduce a dear friend of mine to becoming a public spectacle just to make a point."

Nick looked crushed. "Karen… are you serious? In all the years we have worked together, have you ever **once** seen me give in to sensationalism or any of that other foolishness? I've always taken pride in keeping this show compassionately honest, to help bring about positive changes whenever we can. I can't believe you think I…"

"Stop!" she exclaimed, holding up a hand to silence him. "Of course, I don't believe you would do that! I have no idea why I even suggested such a thing. I guess, over the years, with all she's been through, I've become rather protective of her. It just popped out. I'm so sorry, Nick." *Oh boy… he has that look again…* She smiled and waited.

"That's brilliant! Karen, you're a genius!" Nick stopped pacing long enough to pat her on the shoulder, then resumed his stride while thinking out loud.

"We'll get the Research Department involved and find more patients who have had similar experiences. We'll have them from all over the country, and if they can't come to us, we will go to them. Give them a chance to tell their stories, to have their voices heard. I'll recruit Julie too! I'm sure she would be willing to use her popularity to draw even more attention to the cause. And we'll get Doctor Jensen and other physicians involved, to get them to speak about their side of the situation!"

Karen jumped up, sharing in his excitement. "Nick, those are excellent ideas! This is going to be **big**! Maybe we'll even get the attention of the CDC!"

"Yes!" he exclaimed triumphantly, pumping his fist in the air. "That decides it. From now on July will be Lyme Disease Awareness Month on Peterson's Place, starting **this** July."

"**July**? That doesn't give us a whole lot of time!" Karen pointed out.

"You're right," he agreed, "so we better get started!"

~~~

Julie was obviously in a lot of pain, and Emily seemed incapable of finding anything to do to help. She paced around the room, fiddling with locks of her hair, and watching the *drip drip drip* of the medication running through the tube from the bag into her friend's arm. *This is infuriating! I feel so helpless!*

"Stop beating yourself up," the blonde urged. "It's all part of the process."

Emily looked at her quizzically and repeated, "Part of the process? What do you mean?"

Lowering her eyes guiltily, Julie muttered, "Let's just say that I knew there was a strong likelihood this would happen."

The redhead was still confused. "I don't understand. The first couple of doses, you seemed to be tolerating this process pretty well. But now it looks like your symptoms have gotten worse than they were before you started!"

The model tried to explain, "It looks that way because, in a way, that's what's happening. As if this illness wasn't torturous enough, in the beginning, the treatment can be worse than the disease."

Taking a seat next to the bed, Emily tried again to express her bewilderment. "I don't recall Doctor Jensen telling us about anything like that when he met with me and Anderson after your surgery. What **are** you talking about?"

Fidgeting with the edge of the blanket she was lying under, Julie tried to find the right words. "There's a reason he didn't tell you guys. It's because I **asked** him not to."

"Why would you do that?" The redhead's temper was flaring but she tried to remain calm. "The whole point of him meeting with us was to prepare us for what to expect, so we could help you! What reason could you have for asking him to leave something out that we clearly needed to know?"

Julie sighed and looked at her friend defiantly. "I asked him not to tell either of you because I didn't want you to worry about me any more than you already were. It wasn't **certain** that I would react this way, just **possible**. So, I gambled that it may not come up and you wouldn't need to know."

"Yeah, and how did that work out for ya?" Emily growled.

"Gee, that was helpful," the model groaned.

"Oh, Honey, I'm sorry, I just am not grasping what you're telling me. I still feel like I'm missing something, and I don't know what to do to help you, and I'm very frustrated!"

"Believe me, I know how you feel. Why don't you read this while I switch over to the saline bag? It should help clarify things for you." Julie took a brochure from her nightstand and handed it to her friend.

Emily made herself more comfortable in the chair and began to read silently.

> Lyme disease and other tick-borne diseases are complicated illnesses and because of that, treatment can be complex. Patients who've gone through treatment will often say "symptoms get worse before they get better". One of the reasons for this is a reaction to treatment called a Jarisch-Herxheimer reaction, often shortened just to "Herxheimer" or "herxing". This can happen after a patient starts antibiotic treatment for spirochetal infections like Lyme disease, and tick-borne relapsing-fever. The reaction was first described in 1895 by Adolf Jarisch, an Austrian dermatologist, and later in 1902 by Karl Herxheimer, a German dermatologist. Both doctors documented a pattern of an increase in symptoms shortly after their patients started treatment. (1)

In his book "How Can I Get Better?" Dr. Richard Horowitz describes the Jarisch-Herxheimer (JH) flare as a "temporary worsening of the symptoms of Lyme disease that occurs when the Lyme spirochete is being killed off by antibiotics, creating inflammation. These JH reactions produce cytokines which then create inflammatory symptoms, including increased fever, muscle and joint pain, headaches, cognitive impairment, and a general worsening of the underlying symptomology." (1)

To promote healing, the inflammatory cytokines and the dying bacteria need to be cleared from the body. The more spirochetes that die, the stronger the reaction will be. Ideally, the faster people can clear dead bacteria from their bodies, the sooner they will feel better. This clearing or detoxifying process is commonly known as "detox" with Lyme patients. (1)

The onset for a Lyme herx is generally 48-72 hours after initiating antibiotics and can last for weeks. According to Dr. Joseph Burrascano, Jr., for patients who have chronic or late-stage Lyme, the worst reaction is typically around the fourth week of treatment, very similar to "serum sickness" where one will have a reduction in white blood cells and an increase in liver

enzymes. A strong reaction at week four
indicates ongoing infection. (1)

"Wow, that's a lot to take in," Emily said quietly, laying
the brochure aside. "So, what's happening right now is that
you're herxing?"

Julie adjusted her position in the bed and looked at her
friend. "Yep, I'm one of the many who ends up herxing. But
even though I'm miserable right now, we have to focus on
the fact that this is actually a good thing."

"What? How could extra pain and misery be a good
thing?"

"Think about it! Remember the part you read toward
the end that says 'The more spirochetes that die, the stronger
the reaction will be. Ideally, the faster people can clear dead
bacteria from their bodies, the sooner they will feel better.'
So, my present state of distress tells us the treatment is
working."

Chapter 14

By the time April 14 rolled around, Emily wasn't feeling much like celebrating her birthday. Although she had reached a point where her brain understood what Julie was going through, her heart still ached for her friend. Watching her when she infused through her PICC line was hard, and the herxing was mind-blowing.

On one of Julie's office visits to have the bandage changed, it was discovered that the site where the line entered her arm was slightly infected. Doctor Jensen treated her for it and the infection cleared up fairly quickly, and there had been no other complications. He was pleased with her progress so far and everyone remained hopeful for a positive outcome.

Julie was adjusting to her "new normal" remarkably well. It didn't take long before she became quite adept at handling every step of the infusion process, and she even had a meeting scheduled with her agent later in the month to talk about returning to modeling part-time. While she was admittedly nervous about the future of her career, with her support team's encouragement, she managed to stay in fairly good spirits.

Emily had been spending more time with her father at the office when she wasn't helping Julie. Andrew decided to officially retire at the end of the year, so he was showing his daughter the ropes to prepare her for the day it would all be hers. She was smart, and a fast learner, but thinking of the day when she would be there without her dad by her side made her sad.

The pregnancy was progressing nicely, and she was grateful to be past the stage where she had morning sickness. At her last checkup, Emily and Nick were thrilled to be reassured that the baby was healthy. When the ultrasound showed they were going to have a son, they were ecstatic. They set up the space off their bedroom as a nursery again and were happy that their baby boy would be welcomed home to his sister's old room.

There was so much going on in everyone's lives, and it was hard for Emily to focus on her own happiness when she knew her best friend was suffering. Trying to think about planning a birthday party was more than the mother-to-be wanted to deal with. Julie had invited her over for lunch the Saturday before the big day so the two of them could have a low-key celebration, and that suited the birthday girl just fine.

~~~

"Nick, thank you so much for doing the Lyme series on the show. Once again, you've risen to the occasion and reminded me how amazing you are." Emily was pulling on a breezy lavender dress to wear for her birthday lunch with Julie.

"You need to be **reminded** of how amazing I am?" he teased. Looking as serious as he could, he gazed intently at her and said, "Honey, have you had a relapse? Do I need to call Doctor Michaels? Are you losing your memory again?"

"Oh, stop it! I don't have time for your silliness!" She scolded him but laughed as she said it. "If you make me late, Julie will be mad at you."

"No, she won't. She texted and asked me to get you to take your time because she's not quite ready." *Oops! Way to go Nick! You should try thinking before you speak. Now I've ruined the whole thing!*

His wife eyed him suspiciously and he did his best to look away from her inquiring gaze. "What do you mean, 'she's not quite ready'? It's just a simple lunch at her place for the two of us. She's still tired from her treatment. I **told** her not to go to any trouble. What are you not saying, Nick?"

I wish I hadn't said anything! Okay, I can salvage this. Think, man, think! "I didn't mean anything by it. You know how Julie is. You've been doing so much for her, she just wants to make it nice for **you**, no matter how small and simple it is."

"But if she wasn't ready, why wouldn't she text **me** and ask me to come a little later, instead of texting **you**?"

Gulp. "You know, I wondered the same thing!" he improvised. "Maybe you should ask her that when you get there. Speaking of getting there, I've got to get to the studio! Have fun, Babe. Talk to you later!" He dashed out of the house before he could stick his other foot in his mouth.

~~~

82

"Hi Emily!" Julie exclaimed. "You look beautiful! Come on in!"

"I don't know; do you think I should? I'm not too early, am I?"

The color drained from the blonde's face and she quickly scowled over her shoulder in the direction of the living room. Turning her attention back to her friend, she tried to recover. "Don't be silly! You're right on time!" Opening the door wider, the model motioned for her to enter.

"SURPRISE!" Emily jumped at the greeting, and saw Nick, Anderson, and her parents standing in the living room, which was decorated with festive blue balloons and streamers. There were two banners: one said, "Happy Birthday Emily!" and the other read "Welcome to Your Baby Shower!"

"Julie Paige Chambers, I **knew** you were up to something! And Nick, you almost let the secret out this morning, didn't you?" Emily accused.

"Nick, how could you? You knew I wanted this to be a surprise!" Julie pouted.

"Guilty as charged," he admitted, "but I covered well, didn't I?"

"Oh, what difference does it make?" Anderson chimed in. "Meagan has outdone herself once again and arranged this lovely family event, so let's celebrate Emily and the soon-to-arrive little… What's his name going to be, guys?"

"It **better** be Andrew!" Emily's dad chimed in.

Everyone laughed and managed to save the Petersons from divulging their son's name just yet. They exchanged a wink, then Meagan spoke up. "It's time for gifts!"

Emily opened her birthday presents and Nick took care of the baby gifts. They received some adorable baby things for the nursery, and the birthday girl got some needed maternity clothes. It turned out to be a special day after all.

~~~

"I don't know how to thank you for your patience this past year." Julie was sitting in her agent's office, nervously hoping this meeting would have the result she needed. *If this doesn't go in my favor, I don't know what I'm going to do! My career, my dreams, my livelihood, my insurance to cover treatment… it all hangs on this!*

"It's been **over** a year, but who's counting?" Raven Shackleford sounded as cold and unfriendly as she appeared to anyone who didn't know her.

With her jet black, blunt cut, bobbed hair and bangs, the stern set of her thin lips that were always painted dark red, and her too thin body routinely clothed in black and white with black stilettos, she did present an intimidating vibe, to say the least. Fortunately, Julie and Raven had found a natural rapport from the beginning, and the model saw past all that outer pretense to the heart of the woman inside.

Raven had a well-deserved reputation for being one of the best in the business, and that was often misinterpreted as malice. The truth was, she was far less about intimidation tactics and more about genuine concern for the lives and careers of the models she managed.

Sounding like the version of herself that Julie was accustomed to, Raven asked, "So, what news do you have for me? How are you doing, My Dear?"

Julie proceeded to give her agent a shortened version of what was going on with her, careful to include only the details she felt were relevant to trying to salvage her career. In conclusion, she pleaded, "So, I'm doing better and feel like I'm ready for us to make a plan for me to come back. I hope you understand I'll need to start out part-time, but I believe I can get to the place where I can go full time again… eventually… well… maybe with a few less hours… and a little less traveling…"

Oh, who am I kidding? I've been gone over a year. I have a PICC line in my arm and chest, for Pete's sake! If I was in her 6-inch heels, I'd tell me this idea is absurd!

Chapter 15

"Hello, everyone, and welcome to the show! We have a very special event starting today on Peterson's Place!" Nick was opening the program with an extra level of enthusiasm. "If you're a regular viewer, you know what I'm talking about. And if you're joining us for the first time, you've picked a great day to tune in. It's May, and around here, that means it's Parkinson's Disease Awareness Month!"

The crowd cheered as the cameraman turned his attention from the host and panned slowly across the audience. The studio was packed today, which was an encouraging sign. Once the focus returned to Nick and the applause subsided, he continued.

"We are going to have a great month intended to educate and inform you. We will give you the opportunity daily to donate to the cause and believe me when I say any and all contributions are important and can make a difference! Across the bottom of the screen, you will see a phone number you can call, a website you can visit, and information about how to text in your gift, so there are multiple ways to chip in. I want to say, 'thank you' in advance for your generosity, because I know I can count on my viewers to rise to the occasion!"

More applause gave him a moment to glance stage left and see his special guests waiting in the wings. After seeing their thumbs up signal, he proceeded. "I don't want you to think it's all going to be statistics and data. You're also going to be entertained by some wonderful guests, from famous people you've seen on stage and screen to everyday folks from around the country. All of them have had their lives impacted in one way or another by Parkinson's disease."

Pausing briefly for dramatic flair, he openly looked to the left again, this time with an intentional smile. Turning his attention back to the crowd, he teased, "We'll start with two of those special guests who are here today, waiting just offstage to share their story with you. I can't wait for you to meet them, so let's bring them out… right after this break for a word from our sponsors!"

The audience groaned at the delay in finding out who was there, and the Producer called out "Back in 3!" Nick switched off the microphone clipped to his tie and walked backstage. "Are you ready for this?"

"As ready as we'll ever be," they said in unison.

~~~

Raven had asked Julie to give her some time to think about how to handle the situation regarding her career. The agent kept mulling it over but was having a hard time making a decision. *This is my reputation and Julie's at stake. I sympathize with her situation, and I know the poor girl is going through quite an ordeal, but that's not my problem. I have a business to run. When she first took her leave of absence, it drew quite a bit of media attention. Everyone wanted to know where she was, what was going on and when she'd be back. Then they started speculating and the rumor mill went crazy, which, in this industry, was actually kind of a good thing. At least it kept her name and face in the public eye. But the longer she was gone, the less was said about her absence. I issued periodic press statements about her, weakly promising a comeback I couldn't put a timeframe on...*

Pacing around her elegant office, she stopped at the large picture window and looked out over the city. *I love this view, especially at night. The lights remind me of my early days in New York. I learned so much about the modeling world then and was thrilled when I made enough of a name for myself to come back home to Brentwood Heights and open this agency. I've come a long way since then.*

Turning back to her desk, she drummed her long red nails on the surface, a habit she had when she was trying to make a decision. *My name would be on the line if I bring Julie back! If it didn't work out, I could lose everything I've worked so hard to achieve. I don't know if I'm willing to take that risk!*

Raven walked down the hall to the studio to check on things and be sure the room was ready for the photo shoot scheduled the next day. She also hoped a change of scenery might help bring her a little clarity. When she stepped inside, she looked around at the various sets displayed, the lights and other equipment, and her mind became flooded with memories.

I remember the first day Julie came to see me. She handed me her portfolio, and even though there wasn't much in it yet, she carried herself with so much poise and confidence, as if she was already a top model and would be doing me a favor allowing me to sign her.

With a grin, she strolled around the set and let the recollections continue. *I nervously watched her first test session and I honestly didn't know what to expect. She **nailed** it. She moved like a pro, instinctively knowing how to move her body, yet taking direction when needed. And her photos… oh my, even those first photos were stunning. I knew then she was something special.*

Suddenly everything became clear, and she didn't know why there was ever any doubt. Hurrying back to her office, she perched on the desk and picked up her phone. It seemed it would never stop ringing and she thought she may end up having to leave a message, but finally there was an answer.

"Hi Raven." The voice on the other end sounded nervous.

"Hi, Julie. You better start practicing that beautiful smile of yours, My Dear, because you and I are staging a comeback like the modeling world has never seen!"

~~~

"Ladies and gentlemen, please put your hands together and give a warm Peterson's Place welcome to our special guests today, my father-in-law, Andrew Peters, and my beautiful wife, Emily Peterson!" The studio audience went wild, applauding and cheering as if the two walking onstage were major celebrities.

Unsure how to respond to that kind of attention, they both bowed awkwardly and took their seats.

"Wow, that really was quite a reception!" Nick observed. "Thanks to all of you for making my family feel so accepted. Emily, you look beautiful, as always."

There was subtle laughter across the studio as she blushed and said, "Thank you, Babe."

Next, he addressed her dad. "Andrew, it's so great to have you here today."

"It's an honor, Nick. Thank you so much for doing this to raise awareness and funds, and also for allowing my daughter and me to be your first guests this month."

"Why don't you start us off, Andrew, and tell us about your journey so far."

The distinguished gentleman trembled only mildly as he relayed his story, sharing about the first symptoms, how he hid it from the family, the testing he went through, and how troubled he was when he passed out at the wedding and all of his secrets came out in such a profound way. As he went on to relate the treatments he had tried and how well he was doing now, he decided he should share what he had learned.

"I'll wrap this up by saying how important my family has been to me through this experience. I kept everything bottled up inside in the beginning, telling myself I was protecting them. In reality, that ended up hurting them more. They have been my rock, and I know now they would have been there for me from the start if I had given them that opportunity. So, if you find yourself dealing with this, or any other health crisis, for that matter, my advice is, don't isolate yourself. Having a strong support system is a vital part of an effective treatment plan."

Applause erupted, and Andrew nodded his thanks with a smile. Emily reached over and put her hand on his, and he laced their fingers together. In that moment, he wished Meagan had accepted Nick's invitation to appear on the show as well, but she said it would make her too nervous and she'd be more comfortable in the audience. Looking down at her seated on the front row, he grinned as she blew him a kiss.

"Alright, folks, we have to take another break," Nick announced. "When we come back, my lovely wife will talk to us about what this illness is like for family members and give us some tips on how to handle that."

"Back in 3!" the Producer cried. Once back on the air, Emily shared her side of the story, and throughout the month, both famous and unfamiliar guests appeared and did the same. By month-end, they had raised over sixty thousand dollars for Parkinson's disease research.

Chapter 16

"Anderson, I don't know if I can do this!" It was Julie's first day back to work, and he had stopped by to see her on his way to the hospital because she was about ten times more nervous than she expected to be, which was a lot.

"Julie, we've talked about this. Repeatedly. This is exactly what you wanted and what you fought for! I know you're anxious, and that's understandable, but, Baby, you've **got** this!" He kissed her tenderly then gave her a warm hug. "You are the strongest woman I know, remember?"

She smiled at him and taunted, "Yeah, yeah, yeah, red leaves, blah, blah, blah." Turning her back, she started to walk away, but he pulled her back and started tickling her.

"Blah, blah, blah? This is how you thank me for comparing your strength to the most beautiful leaves known to man? How dare you, young lady!" He continued to tickle and tease, knowing the endorphins released would help elevate Julie's mood.

Sunlight played in through the window and reflected off the engagement ring. He held up her hand so they both could see it. "Are you going to be able to wear this in your photos?" He had wondered before, so decided to ask.

"They won't have a choice, as far as I'm concerned," she insisted. "I'm sure not going to take it off."

"**There's** the determination I was looking for!" her fiancé exclaimed. "I knew my tough girl was still in there!"

Fiddling with the PICC line on her arm, she began questioning again. "How am I supposed to try to look fierce and beautiful with this thing sticking out of me?"

He looked at her adoringly. "You don't have to **try** to be fierce **or** beautiful, Honey. You're both of those things and more **without** trying."

Throwing her arms around him, she almost knocked him down, then planted a long kiss on his lips. "What was that for?" he asked when he could breathe again.

"That, my dear fiancé, was for always being there for me, for putting up with my doubts but not letting me give in to them, and for generally being the best human being I've ever met."

"Wow… I don't know about all that, Julie. That's a lot to live up to…" He just couldn't resist the sarcasm because he knew it would make her laugh.

"Oh, but you're strong! You can do it! You're red leaves!" She giggled as she headed for the door and grabbed her keys. Adjusting the photo of Anderson that was back in its place on the console table, she kissed the real man goodbye and said, "Have a good day treating patients, Doctor. I have to go be fierce, now."

Following her out of the apartment, he watched her walk to her car and shook his head. *My gosh, I love that woman. I can't wait to make her my wife.*

~~~

93

The other models, the photographer and Raven were all waiting for Julie when she arrived at the studio. "Welcome back!" They all greeted her with applause, making her feel much better. *Being accepted by my colleagues is the first hurdle to my comeback.*

"Thanks, everybody! This is quite a welcoming committee!" There were hugs and handshakes all around, then it was time for hair and make-up. It had been so long since she could just relax and have someone pamper her, so Julie enjoyed the luxury.

Raven stood by the chair trying to stay out of the make-up artist's way while she reviewed the plan for the day. "Okay, Julie, everyone has been briefed about the situation as we discussed. They understand and are more than willing to make any necessary accommodations to make this shoot work."

"I don't want any special treatment, I just want to model again," Julie insisted. "I don't want my... situation... to interrupt the process."

"Oh, pooh, don't be ridiculous. It's not all about you, Darling," Raven mocked with an uncharacteristic grin. "Now listen. We have you posing in a group today for a reason. You will be positioned so the other girls block your arm, and the cut of your outfit covers the port on your chest. All you have to do is..."

"Be fierce!" Julie exclaimed. "Yes, my personal coach has been drilling that in my head all morning."

"Well, good, because he's absolutely right!" Her agent knew the coach was Anderson, and the model had filled her in about how supportive he was.

"Now, about this ring..." She took the blonde's left hand and held it out, admiring the beauty of the sparkler. Before she could finish her sentence, she felt that hand being pulled from her grasp.

"Don't get any ideas, Raven, the ring stays! Non-negotiable."

"Well, of course it does, Dear. Want to know the first rule of a big comeback?"

"Okay, I'll bite. What's the first rule of a big comeback?" Julie asked.

"Create **mystery**, Honey! We **want** people to see that ring! Let them wonder! Let them **talk**! If they're talking about the ring, they're talking about **you**, and that's a splendid thing!" Raven flitted away with a satisfied smile and the pro applied the final touches to Julie's lip gloss.

The photo shoot went even better than everyone had hoped. Anyone who didn't know her would never suspect that Julie was in the fight of her life, and the photos were astounding. The client had taken a risk allowing Raven to include a model who had been away from the industry for over a year, but when they saw the end result, they would be thrilled they took that chance.

~~~

"I knew you could do it, Baby! And before you say anything, no, I don't mean that in an 'I told you so' kind of way. I mean it in an 'I never doubted you because you're amazing' kind of way." Anderson was back at Julie's place, making dinner for her while she rested and did her infusion for the day.

"Thanks for the support, but the clarification wasn't necessary. I'm way too tired to argue with you." She was set up on the couch with a comfy pillow behind her back so she had to speak up so he could hear her from the kitchen, and even raising her voice required more energy than she had right now.

He walked in and set up two TV trays so they could watch a movie and relax while they ate. "No arguments, Doctor's orders." He kissed her forehead and went back to get their plates. He brought back a dish of whole wheat pasta with marinara sauce and placed it on the tray in front of her, along with a napkin, fork, and large spoon for twirling.

"You take such good care of me," she praised. "I think I should keep you around. You're pretty handy."

"Oh, is **that** why you agreed to marry me? Because I'm handy?" he teased.

"That, and other reasons," Julie said with a grin. As he left the room again, she called out, "Speaking of marrying you, we need to get to work on wedding plans. October will be here before we know it."

Coming back in with his own food and essentials, he took a seat next to his fiancée on the couch and replied, "I've been thinking about that. You have so much going on, what would you think about asking Meagan to help out with the wedding? With Andrew getting ready to retire in December, he's spending so much time with Emily preparing her to take over the insurance company, I have the impression that Meagan is, well, at loose ends. She does such a beautiful job with events, food, flowers… I think she would be great at planning our wedding."

Julie gazed at Anderson for so long, he was starting to wonder if she hated the idea. Finally, she said, "That. Is. **Brilliant**! Since my own mother isn't here to help, I just assumed I was going to have to lean on Emily a lot, but with her being pregnant and training to take over for her dad, I wasn't feeling good about that. I don't know why it didn't occur to me to ask her mom! See, there's **another** reason I keep you around. You have great ideas!"

Shaking his head and chuckling, he settled back in beside her. "I feel so used. It's a good thing you're beautiful," he teased sarcastically.

The couple enjoyed the pasta and the romantic comedy they decided to watch. Although happily exhausted from the long and demanding day, Julie felt primarily satisfied. She had everything she could hope for, and life was good.

Chapter 17

"Emily, you really should let me help with this. You're eight months pregnant; it's too much!" Meagan tried to reason with her daughter.

"Mom, please. I'm pregnant, not incapacitated. You have enough going on already with Julie's wedding. Thank you again for helping her, by the way." The redhead stretched and rubbed her lower back as she looked around at the patio area. Once again, the traditional red, white, and blue banners and streamers were hung, and festive plans were in full swing for the July 4th neighborhood picnic. It made her happy.

"I was delighted that she asked me. I'm having so much fun, I may have to start advertising my party planning services!" Her mother was only joking, but the wheels began turning in her daughter's mind.

"That's a great idea, Mom! You could open your own business! You would be so great at that! Everybody knows how talented you are and…"

Shaking her head, the older woman nipped that suggestion in the bud in a hurry. "My Dear, that is absolutely out of the question."

Emily had been moving from table to table, placing centerpieces made of votive candles in glass cups surrounded by flags. At her mother's refusal of her idea, she stopped and asked, "Why not? You would likely be very successful!"

"Right as your father is retiring? No, thank you. If I wanted my own business, I would have done it years ago! I enjoy planning dinner parties and such, but I do it for fun, not profit. I only accepted Julie's offer as a favor, to be of help to her, and to take pressure off you."

Thinking about it for a minute, her daughter understood. "I get that, Mom. I wasn't thinking. I guess I just don't want you to get bored."

"Bored?" she exclaimed with an incredulous laugh. "My husband is soon to be home every day, and even sooner we'll welcome our grandson into the world! How could I **possibly** have time to get **bored**?"

The women giggled together, and Meagan insisted Emily sit down and relax with a cold drink. It was still morning, but the temperature was already climbing, and the humidity wasn't helping. The mother-to-be finally agreed to take a break and settled herself in a chair by the pool with a glass of iced water. Watching her mom finish up with the centerpieces made her smile.

There are so many memories around this pool. Some are good and some aren't, but it has all turned out quite well. Everyone has come a long way, and although we've endured some tragedies, now our hearts are full of joy. Dad's doing well, Mom gets to have him home in a few months, Julie's life is back on track and she's getting married, and Nick and I will soon be parents again!

~~~

"We have a special surprise in store today, folks! As you may know, Peterson's Place had great success with our Parkinson's Awareness month in May. Continuing in that tradition, today we are starting a new series on the show, declaring July as Lyme Disease Awareness Month." Nick paused for the audience applause in response.

"The illness is different, but our purpose is the same, and just as critical. I can tell you, in doing research for this, I have learned some shocking and heart-breaking things. Much of what you're going to hear this month will make you cry. It will make you **angry**. Hopefully, it will move you to take action. We'll get into this complicated and often controversial disease right after this break."

During the commercial, Nick switched off his mic and ducked backstage, as he was prone to do. "Are you ready, Julie? I'll be introducing you soon after we resume."

"I'm as ready as I can be, Nick. I'll be honest, I'm nervous. I've never talked so publicly about this, and it's scary. This isn't just personal for me. Public response can affect my career." The model kept shifting her weight, clearly agitated.

"I have to get back out there," the host said hurriedly. "You've got this. I have faith in you!"

He returned to his mark just in time. "Welcome back to Peterson's Place! If you're just joining us, I want to let you know we're launching a new series for this month about Lyme disease. I started this journey because a dear family friend is fighting her own Lyme battle right now. She's here with us today, and I will introduce her to you in a few minutes." There were cheers from the crowd, who always seemed to get excited about guests, even before they found out who they were.

Nick continued. "I knew practically nothing about Lyme disease a short time ago, and I would bet most of you don't know much about it, either, because it isn't talked about nearly enough. When I decided to call attention to it, I knew I had much to learn, but I had **no idea** what I was in for. As I said at the top of the show, I've found out some very distressing things in this process." A quiet rumbling of reaction rolled through the audience.

"For example, Lyme disease is one of the fastest growing infectious diseases in the country, and one of the most difficult to diagnose. Experts in the medical and scientific community, as well as key legislators, have deemed Lyme disease to be an **epidemic**… a national public health **crisis**… and a **growing** threat." (1) Gasps could be heard throughout the studio, then it got noticeably quiet.

"**New** tick-borne diseases are emerging, the number of tick endemic regions is **growing**, the tick population is increasing, and the number of people infected with Lyme disease is steadily **rising**. The Centers for Disease Control and Prevention (CDC) report that at least **300,000** people are infected with Lyme disease **each year, just** in the United States alone. That's not even considering patients in the rest of the world. Folks, that's **25,000 new** cases per **month**." (1) More cries of alarm got louder around the room.

"That's right, you're shocked, aren't you? So was I. That's why I knew I had to do something, to bring as much attention as possible to this epidemic and the plight of those suffering in its painful grasp." Scattered applause could be heard.

"It is **imperative** that physicians are thoroughly educated in the complexity of Lyme disease and trained in identifying it and providing effective treatment plans!" (1) That brought a standing ovation, and Nick knew his message was getting through.

When the fanfare settled down, he moved on. "Ladies and gentlemen, we will have a live satellite interview a little later in the show with someone I'm anxious to introduce you to, but my first guest today is here in the studio with us. She's a dear friend of my wife's and has also become a good friend of mine. But guess what? You all know and love her, too!" He paused as people whispered amongst themselves, wondering who it could be.

"She's been out of the limelight for the past year, and now she's ready to share her story about why. It's one you'll find hard to believe, but I can personally assure you, everything you're going to hear is true. Please put your hands together and give a very warm welcome to Miss Julie Chambers!"

As the model walked out onstage waving, the crowd went wild. On their feet again, they clapped and cheered, looking at each other in disbelief. It was more than she could have hoped for. Taking a seat in the chair reserved for guests, she smiled her thanks as the ovation continued.

She blew kisses to the kind audience members, then politely motioned for quiet. If they kept it up, there would be no time for her interview! Once they simmered down, Nick turned to Julie. "What a welcome! Julie, how did that feel?"

"Nick, such an enthusiastic response was unexpected, and truly appreciated!" Facing front, she blew a kiss again and said, "Thank you all so much!"

"Julie, I know you've had concerns about going public with what you've been through. I want to tell you how grateful I am that you're here today, and that you've granted me your first live interview. I realize this is not an easy thing to do."

"No, it isn't, Nick. Talking about such a personal thing is uncomfortable, to say the least. When you first approached me, I wasn't sure I could do this," the model admitted. "However, if sharing my story can help other people like me get help, then it's completely worth it. So, thank **you**, Nick, for giving me this opportunity." More applause from the audience reaffirmed she made the right decision.

Watching the show from home, Emily beamed with pride and rubbed her swollen belly. *Look at that, Little One. Your daddy and my best friend, on live TV, are out there changing the world.*

Chapter 18

Julie walked gracefully into the lobby of Black Raven Modeling Agency. It was a hot August day, but she looked cool as a cucumber in her light green silk sheath and yellow high-heeled sandals. The flutter sleeves on the dress flowed just to her elbow, long enough to cover the port in her arm. She had chosen a yellow necklace and simple earrings to complete the look, and she was stunning.

Since starting IV treatment several months ago, her progress had been even better than she and Doctor Jensen had dared to hope. Her infusion therapy was even less frequent now, and she had lined up several future magazine print jobs since her first one turned out so well. She wasn't sure why Raven asked her to come in today, but she was hoping it was for even more good news.

"Hi, Miss Chambers," the receptionist greeted her cheerfully. "Ms. Shackleford has gotten delayed on a conference call, but she asked me to let you know she'll be with you in a few minutes."

"Okay, that's fine. Thanks for the information, Charity." The blonde turned to have a seat but was stopped by the pretty young staff member.

"Oh, Miss Chambers? I just want to tell you how **wonderful** it is to have you back. We've all missed you around here! And congratulations on your engagement!"

Wow, it still feels like home. It's almost like I never left. "Charity, all of that sentiment is greatly appreciated. Thank you so much!"

"Julie, you're looking very well." Raven entered the lobby and greeted her model with her typically cool persona, but once the two of them were behind the closed door of the agent's office, she took Julie's hands in hers.

"**You**, My Dear, are brilliant. I must say, it would have been nice of you to run it by **me** first, but still… **brilliant**!" Raven released her hold and waved her hands in the air like jazz hands. She was obviously very happy about something, but Julie had no idea what she was referring to.

"Um… thank you?" She stammered. "I appreciate the compliment, but what are you talking about?"

"What am I talking about? Your surprise appearance on Peterson's Place! **That's** what I'm talking about! That kind of exposure… I couldn't have planned a better comeback tactic if I tried! But why didn't you talk to me about it first?"

Uh oh… am I in trouble here? "It happened rather quickly, Raven. Nick didn't give me a whole lot of notice. Honestly, I really didn't think about it, but I suppose I should have. I'm not in some sort of contract violation or something, am I?"

"Oh, no, no, nothing like that. No legal problems here. You know me; I just don't like not being in the loop. But right now, I don't even care about that. Julie, my phones have been ringing off the hook! Every client who ever worked with you wants you back, and some who haven't given us the time of day before can't wait to book you now!"

"Wait… **what**? Am I hearing you right?" *This can't be!*

"Yes, yes, My Dear, you heard me! I know you're still in treatment, **and** you're planning your wedding, **and** you and that hot fiancé of yours will be house hunting before long… but how soon do you think we can get you back on the runway?"

Julie jumped to her feet, then had to sit back down because she stood up too fast and almost fainted. "**Runway**? I don't know about that, Raven. Print ads with strategically placed props are one thing, but… runway? I can't do live shows with this ugly thing sticking out of my arm… and look at the port in my chest! No designer is going to want that!"

"Au, contraire, my blonde beauty! That's what one would think, but one would be mistaken!" The blackbird had a flair for the dramatic.

"Now you're speaking in riddles again," Julie complained. "Please just be straight with me and tell me what's going on." She adjusted her position in the comfortable chair and waited for an explanation.

"Oh, alright, just take all the fun out of it, why don't you?" Raven sighed, then continued. "You made quite an impression telling your story on that TV talk show. No matter what you may think, it took an extraordinarily strong woman with a lot of moxie to do what you did, and now everybody wants to get in on the cause."

The model gasped. "Get in on the cause? What does that mean? Are there clients that want to… get involved?"

"Yes!" Raven exclaimed triumphantly.

"But… this is the fashion industry… where perfection is everything! I don't understand." It seemed too good to be true.

"I am telling you, several of the top designers in the biz are putting together a fashion show to raise funds for and promote awareness about Lyme disease. They are bringing in all the top models, and the primary focus will be on **you**!"

Julie's head was spinning. *Wow… I was hoping for good news, but **this**? I never would have dreamed of something like this!* "Wait a minute; slow down. When is this event supposed to happen? I'm getting married October 2nd!"

"No problem! That's the beauty of it!" The woman was in full blown agent mode. "The show isn't until October 27th! You will have plenty of time!"

"This all sounds… amazing… but I don't know…" About that time, Julie's phone buzzed. Pulling it from her purse, she saw a text from Nick: [911-IT'S TIME!]

~~~

Emily's labor went quickly and fairly easily. By the time Julie got there, she almost missed it. Rushing into the waiting room, she met up with Andrew and Meagan.

"This is so exciting!" she squealed, hugging each of them.

Nobody had mentioned Sarah Beth or what happened years ago, but Julie gave voice to what they had all been thinking. "There are no complications, right?"

"We don't know," Meagan replied nervously. "We haven't heard anything yet."

Just then Anderson arrived and joined the little group. It wasn't long before a nurse came and told them they could all go in, but only for a few moments.

The parents looked up and saw everyone come in to see the baby. They were all smiles as they proudly introduced their newborn son. "Hey, so glad you all made it to share this day with us. This is our **healthy** little boy, Andrew Stanley Peterson."

Andrew's breath caught and a tear escaped. "Oh, my, you named him after **both** your dads. That's perfect. **He's** perfect."

Meagan touched the infant's cheek and smiled. "He's beautiful!" she cried.

"Yes... yes, he is!" Emily and Nick agreed together. "We'll call him Drew."

The door to the room opened again and their favorite nurse, Faye Gordon, crept in. "Good evening, everyone! It's nice to see all of you here under such **happy** circumstances this time!"

They all expressed greetings then turned their attention back to Drew. Faye moved to get a closer look. "I just had to sneak in and see this boy! He's a sweet little miracle!"

Emily smiled at the nurse's delight then asked, "How did you know we were here, Faye?"

Nick piped up, "I bet I know the answer to that! It was that nosy Marlayna, wasn't it? She makes it her business to find out and then blab everything that happens around here." Checking his watch, he continued, "It's about time for her to show up to take over for you."

The nurse stepped back and announced with a big smile, "Actually, no, I didn't hear it from her. I saw your names on the delivery room schedule."

"Oh, that makes sense. Just keep her out of here, please," Emily begged.

"That won't be a problem," the nurse assured her.

"How can you be so sure?" Nick asked.

"It's quite simple. You see, Marlayna doesn't work here anymore!" Faye's smile was bright as the sun.

"What?"

"You're kidding!"

"How did that happen?"

As usual, they were all talking at once. Faye motioned for everyone to quiet down, for the sake of the baby. "Let's just say she overstepped her boundaries one too many times!" She bid them goodbye with a promise to check back in later.

"Well, how about that?" Andrew remarked. "This is **truly** a perfect day!"

Chapter 19

"You'll never guess what happened!" Anderson rushed in the door at Julie's place, hurrying right past her in the process. He was clearly excited about something. "It just came on the market, so we're going to have to take action fast!"

Motioning for Julie to have a seat beside him on the couch, he shoved his tablet toward her a couple of times. Looking at him and laughing, she took the device and said, "Calm down, Babe! You're acting like a kid with a new toy."

"I can't help it! This house has everything we're looking for, and it's in the neighborhood we want. It's even in our price range! Remember that brick ranch style we kept looking at and wishing it was for sale?"

Now Julie was the one eager to check it out. "Really? The one with the wide wrap-around front porch? You're not kidding with me, are you? Because if you are, that's just mean! You know how much I like that house!"

"Honey, would I rush over here this early on a Saturday morning acting like a fool just to pull a joke on you? The ad is already open there on the screen, if you'll just look!" He pointed at the tablet enthusiastically, urging her to focus.

Scrolling through the generous array of photos, they found each one to be as promising as the last. The house featured an open floor plan that included a large family room with a fireplace, a dining room big enough to host some nice dinners, and a modern kitchen they both dreamed of cooking in together. Beautiful hardwood floors gleamed throughout, and the brushed nickel hardware and appliance accents were exactly what they wanted.

At the back of the home they discovered three spacious bedrooms, one of which was an impressive master suite. Tray ceilings, an alcove with a window seat, and two generous walk-in closets completed the design. The final pictures showed a stunning en suite bathroom with separate tub and shower, marble countertops, dual sinks, and heated floors. It made for the perfect retreat at the end of a long day.

They talked about furniture placement, what style of decor they wanted, and even how beautiful a Christmas tree would look in the front window. It was no surprise they shared similar tastes, and they already knew they liked everything they had learned about the neighborhood from looking at other houses in that area. There was no doubt this was the home they had been dreaming of.

Anderson quickly dialed the number listed for the real estate agent. He couldn't believe it when she answered on the second ring and agreed to show them the property later that afternoon. When he ended the call, the couple squealed like a couple of kids, then hugged it out over their good fortune.

"This works out perfectly," Julie said. "I'm getting together with Meagan this morning to go over some wedding details and try on my dress again. Then I will meet you and the realtor at the house afterward."

Jumping to his feet, Anderson replied, "That sounds great. I have a patient to see this morning, but I'll be done in plenty of time. Hey, I just had an idea. Do you think Meagan would be interested in helping decorate our new place?"

His fiancée giggled at his childlike excitement. "Oh, Mr. Blair, you're something else. First of all, it's not our place yet, and secondly, Meagan has already done so much toward the wedding, I don't know…"

He interrupted her by taking her in his arms. "**First** of all, future **Mrs.** Blair, have a little faith. It **will** be our house! And secondly, just ask her, okay?"

"Yes, Dear," she replied mockingly. "Hey, I like the sound of that… the future Mrs. Blair."

"I do, too. I can't wait to see you in that dress!" he said with a smile.

"You know the rules, Mister. You **have** to wait. It's tradition." She replied firmly. *When he **does** see me, I hope to knock his socks off!*

"Oh, tradition, schmition," Anderson pouted. "Since when are we traditional?"

She kissed him tenderly, then pushed him away. "You better get to work and stop arguing with me!"

"Yes, Dear," he laughed.

"Oh, and **Doctor** Blair, try to calm down on the way so you don't overdo it with your patient and leave them in worse shape than when they started!"

~~~

"Oh my, Julie, it's such a lovely house! How serendipitous that it's for sale now, and that Anderson saw the listing right away!" Meagan was studying the photos almost as intently as the couple themselves had. "You know, a Christmas tree would display beautifully in that front window!"

With a chuckle, the blonde agreed. "We said the same thing! It's unanimous!" Taking a seat at the kitchen table and sipping the cup of coffee Meagan had given her, she continued cautiously. "Um, I want to ask you something… well, Anderson actually suggested I ask… but you're already doing so much…"

"For goodness sake, child, stop beating around the bush. What is it?" The older woman's motherly voice warmed Julie's heart, but also made her miss her own mom.

I can't wait to see my parents again! It's been too long.

"Well, since my folks won't be here until right before the wedding, and there's already so much going on between now and then, we were wondering… I mean, obviously, we don't have the house yet, but we're hoping, and if it works out… it would mean a lot to us if you could… find the time… if you'd be willing… to help us decorate it… please?"

Taking the young lady's hand, Meagan replied, "Now then, did you have to make that so hard? Goodness gracious, one would think you were asking for money."

They both laughed, then the older woman asked, "Do you want to hear something else funny?"

Julie nodded and Meagan grinned with a wink. "If you had not asked, I was going to offer to help anyway. I'd be delighted!"

"Oh, thank you! This is all so exciting! Okay, deep breath, I have to back burner everything about the house until this afternoon. First things first! Thank you again for letting us have the ceremony here. With all the mature trees, it's a lovely place for a Fall wedding!" She looked at her engagement ring and squealed.

"You're so welcome, of course, Dear. We're in exceptionally good shape, really. The chairs and decorations are scheduled to be delivered and set up in the backyard the day before the ceremony. The arrangements are all made for the cake, flowers, music, and the minister. We have most everything done, really, so let's try on the dress again. I adjusted the sleeves like we talked about, so I think it's going to fit better now." She followed Julie into the guest bedroom where her gown hung on the closet door.

Gazing at the garment lovingly, the bride-to-be's face lit up. She had tried it on a couple of times before, but this time, when she felt the fabric gently flow over her body and looked at herself in the full-length mirror, she became emotional. "Oh, Meagan, it's perfect."

The long ivory silk fit her like a glove. The design was low-cut in the back and had a short train. The front was cut just high enough to cover the port over her heart. The opaque sleeves flowed elegantly to her wrists, concealing the PICC line while still looking stylish.

I may be advocating for Lyme disease, and I'm thankful for the platform I have that enables me to do that. Consequently, it's no secret now that I have this awkward tubing attached to me, but that doesn't mean I want it on display on my wedding day. Thankfully, Raven helped find this extraordinary dress that will help me look and feel more like a healthy bride on our special day.

Suddenly a random pain shot through her back, a not-so-subtle reminder that her body was feeling stressed. *I should have known that was coming. Between the wedding*

*plans, getting back to work, Emily's baby, looking for a house…
it's all positive, happy changes, but still too many at once. This
body doesn't appreciate that and isn't shy about letting me know
when it's time to take a break.*

Doing a few gentle stretches helped somewhat, but she
wasn't about to let it ruin the great day she was having. She
decided counting her blessings would be a good idea. *How
did I get so lucky? Other than battling this wicked disease, I'm
getting everything I ever wanted!*

Chapter 20

"Anderson Blair, put me down! What do you think you're doing?" Julie liked being in his arms, but this was weird. "I know I have issues, but I'm not an invalid."

"If you would stop fighting me, I'm **trying** to carry you over the threshold!" he exclaimed defensively, but he put her down as she asked.

Her blonde hair fell across her eyes as she shook her head in disbelief. "You're supposed to do that on our wedding day, Silly. We aren't married yet." She moved the hair back in place and smiled at him.

"Who says we can't break tradition? Or better yet, start a new one of our own? If I want to carry my fiancée over the threshold on the day we start moving into our house, I will!"

With that, he scooped her up again before she could protest any further and stepped proudly into their new empty living room. Julie couldn't help herself and started giggling like a schoolgirl. "Oh, Babe, I almost can't believe it! Is this beautiful house **really** ours?"

"Maybe I should pinch you and see if you're dreaming!" He sat her on her feet gently, then proceeded to tickle and playfully pinch her. She kept laughing even more, then took his hand and they ran through every room in the house.

When they got to the master bedroom, Anderson pulled her into his arms for a quick kiss.

"How did I ever get so blessed to have a woman like you fall in love with a mess like me?" He kissed the end of her nose impulsively, partly because it was such a cute nose, and partly because he knew it would make her smile.

"Are you kidding? I'm the one who's a mess. Look at this thing." Julie pulled away from him and pointed at the PICC line in her arm. "And this one," she indicated the port in her chest. "I know I shouldn't complain, and I'm really not, it's just so…"

"Beautiful? Life-affirming? **Temporary**?" he interrupted.

"I was going to say 'hideous'… but when you put it that way, I guess I can downgrade it to… unsightly… disagreeable… inconvenient." She lowered her eyes, feeling a little embarrassed for grumbling.

Gently placing his finger under her chin, Anderson tilted her face until she would look at him again. "I understand all those things, Honey, and I'm sorry that you're going through this. But I'm telling you, Doctor Jensen knows what he's doing, and you're going to be so much better off when this treatment is done."

"Oh, I know that," she agreed. "I don't doubt Doctor Jensen or this regimen of care, and I'm already doing better. I just… I don't know how to say this without sounding vain… I'm used to being known and… well, valued… for my appearance. It's a layer of this process I had not anticipated, having to alter my image of myself."

He pulled her in close and held her for a moment, then responded, "I didn't realize you were feeling this way, Babe. I guess for someone in your profession, those thoughts would tend to cross your mind. But, Sweetheart, you don't have to **change** anything. You're just as beautiful as you've always been!" He pointed to the line and the port and continued, "Like I said, these are temporary, and, quite frankly, they're necessary. But they don't change **who** you are or how **gorgeous** you are. Look at this fashion show coming up next month! The designers and sponsors put that whole event together because of **you**!"

"The two of you are the sweetest couple!" Meagan's voice interrupted the romance of their moment, but Julie took a second to repay the charm and kissed the end of Anderson's nose too, as a way of letting him know she appreciated his support.

"I should have known I'd find you hiding out back here," Meagan teased. "Sorry to cut your flirtation short, but I wanted to tell you the moving company has just arrived!"

As Julie grabbed the older woman's hands, they squealed and began to dance around joyfully. Anderson stepped back and looked at them like they were both crazy, then said, "Oh, why not? Looks like fun!" They all laughed together as he whirled into the circle with them. This joyful scene was how the moving men found them.

"Uh… excuse us ma'ams… sir… Where would you like this dresser?"

~ ~ ~

By mid-afternoon, the spacious house was full of furniture, and Anderson had reluctantly gone to his office to see a patient. Meagan was busily unpacking the decor and accessories they had ordered ahead of time. Julie felt like a kid on Christmas morning waiting to look at everything they had chosen, but she tried to stay out of the way until Meagan could check her lists against the shipments and make sure everything they bought had been delivered.

Next the two women gathered the assortment of wedding gifts that had been arriving for the engaged couple. Finally, they could get on with the best part of the move: nesting! Taking advantage of Meagan's designer's eye and Julie's knack for organization, they got to work setting up the kitchen, making beds, arranging closets, and putting all the beautiful decor in place.

"Wow! This place looks incredible!" Emily's excitement was unrestrained when she arrived with enough pizza and sodas to feed a small army. "Mom, you truly are gifted at this interior design thing! Is there even anything left for me to help do?"

Her friend finished putting the last of the drinking glasses in a kitchen cabinet and rushed over to greet her. "Hey, I had a little something to do with all this too, you know! And yes, there's plenty left to do." Julie took some of the pizza boxes and helped carry everything to the dining table. "Thank you bunches for all this food, but why did you bring so much? Did you think the movers would still be here?"

With a mischievous gleam in her eye and a crafty smile on her lips, Emily replied, a little louder than seemed necessary, "I wasn't sure if the moving guys would be around or not, but I did know of some other people who would be here."

"Surprise!" Cathy and Ron Chambers exclaimed, suddenly appearing in the entryway, then rushing into their daughter's welcoming arms. Nobody had even noticed that Emily left the door standing open when she arrived.

"Mom! Dad! I can't believe you're here! I thought you weren't coming until next week!" Julie turned to her best friend and accused, "You knew about this?"

"I was sworn to secrecy! I couldn't tell you, under penalty of Chambers law!"

Suddenly the company of friends grew again as Andrew and Anderson walked in, followed by Nick carrying baby Drew. The allure of the new house temporarily faded as everyone crowded around to welcome Ron and Cathy back to town and to admire the adorable baby.

Once the commotion settled down, Julie and Meagan gave everybody the grand tour. "I can't get over how much you ladies accomplished after I left!" Anderson said. "This place looks like we've lived here for months!"

"It's remarkable, Sweetheart," Cathy complimented. "Meagan, thanks so much for all of your help with the house and the wedding. You always did have a special, magic touch!"

"I don't know about the rest of you, but I'm hungry! Let's eat!" Nick declared unapologetically. Handing out paper plates and napkins his thoughtful wife had the foresight to bring, he opened the pizza boxes while Emily put ice in plastic cups and filled the soda requests.

The eight of them gathered around the dining table, and Julie finally had a chance to ask the question that had been on her mind ever since her parents arrived. "I'm thrilled you guys are here early, but how did that happen? What's going on?"

Ron spoke up first. "The progress on the school we were helping to build has been remarkable. There were more volunteers than anticipated, so the work has been done quicker."

"That's great news! It's wonderful to hear so many people showed up for the cause. So, does this mean that the project is completed? Where are you going next?" Julie inquired.

She noticed her parents exchanging glances with everyone around the table. Then each person got a secretive smile on their face. *Hmm, it's obvious they all know something I don't. Why do I get the feeling there's more to this trip than just being here for the wedding?* "Okay, what's going on? What am I missing?"

Her mom clapped her hands together and announced, "We're home to stay!"

As always, the group started talking at once. Julie sat back, happily taking it all in. *I need to count my blessings again, but I'm not sure I can count that high!*

Chapter 21

"You look absolutely breathtaking!" Emily told the bride as she adjusted the wreath of autumn flowers and baby's breath Julie had chosen to wear instead of a traditional veil. "Anderson is going to keel over when he sees you!"

"I sure hope not! I'd like him to be conscious when we take our vows!"

"Yes, I suppose it wouldn't be legal if he wasn't!"

The best friends giggled like a couple of kids, then calmed down and stood gazing at their reflection in the cheval mirror. Emily's muted coral maid of honor dress looked as lovely on her as the ivory bridal gown was on Julie. Both fought back tears as memories of all they had experienced together went through their minds.

"Emily, do you remember our Senior prom?" Julie reminisced.

"How could I forget?" the redhead groaned. "We had such great expectations for that night, and boy, did those high hopes get dashed!"

"Our dates were late, they didn't bring us flowers, neither of them could dance and they took us home early!" The blonde recounted the unpleasant evening.

"Actually, I think they took us home early because we asked them to!" Emily added. "The highlight of our Prom was the two of us eating popcorn together in our pjs and staying up late watching romantic comedies."

"That's right," the model agreed. "We've always been there for each other."

They hugged and her maid of honor was reminded of the presence of the ports, cleverly hidden by the design of her wedding gown. "How's your treatment going? You have still been pretty stoic about it all, even after you revealed the whole story."

"I'm doing well," Julie answered. "The herxing has pretty much stopped, I'm thinking more clearly, the pain level has decreased. I mean, I may never be quite 'normal', but I'm definitely better than I was, and improving a little more every week. I'm so thankful Doctor Michaels introduced me to Doctor Jensen!"

"So am I!" Emily exclaimed. "I shudder to think how much worse you could have gotten."

"Let's not even go there," the bride said. "Today is all about happiness!"

"Oh, my goodness, look at our stunning girls!" Cathy declared proudly as both moms arrived to help with last-minute preparations.

Meagan gasped when she caught a glimpse of the younger ladies. "You're right, they are stunning!" She agreed, then turned her attention to the bride. "Do you need anything or does my daughter have every detail covered, as I suspect she does?"

"We're good to go!" Julie declared. "Let's do this!"

~~~

Meagan had recruited the rest of the family to assist with various details, and all of them contributed to making Julie and Anderson's wedding elegant and pretty, yet low key and simple. The trees in the Peters' back yard boasted a splendid array of green, yellow, orange and red. There was an explosion of color, but oh, those brilliant reds! Even the foliage honored the bride on this memorable day.

At the couple's request, the gathering was an intimate one with only family and a small number of friends present. At one end of the garden, a trellis covered in coral and yellow roses served as the altar, and chairs for the guests were scattered around at random to maintain the casual mood. The center aisle was covered with rose petals that matched the altar, and soft instrumental music played through the speakers placed around the perimeter of the yard.

"Are you ready?" Nick asked Anderson as he adjusted the groom's tie. They were off to the side with the minister, waiting for their cue.

"I've never been more ready for anything!" his friend replied. "Thanks again for being my best man. After all we've been through, it means a lot to me."

"We have come a long way, that's for sure!" Nick agreed.

Just then the entry music began, and the officiant said, "That's us."

"Let's do this!" whispered Anderson, and the three of them took their places in front of the trellis.

Right inside the back door, the small bridal party waited their turn to emerge. "Daddy, I'm so happy you're here to walk me down the aisle, and even happier you and Mom have moved back home to stay. My heart is full of gratitude and joy today!"

With a smile reserved only for his daughter, Ron said, "Knowing **you** are happy makes me and your mother happy. Anderson is a wonderful man, and we're thrilled for both of you."

"Okay, you two, before you make me cry, I'm walking!" Emily joked. Opening the door slightly, she listened for her prompt, then stepped out when the music started.

"It's just us now, Sweetheart," Ron said. He offered Julie his arm and invited, "Shall we?"

Feeling too emotional to speak, his daughter slipped one hand through the crook of her dad's arm and held onto her Fall bouquet with the other. The wedding march began to play and together they took the first step toward her future.

~~~

I can't believe she is about to become my wife! When Anderson saw Julie walking down the aisle, that was all he could think. *She's so beautiful, smart, and kind. I still don't know how I got so lucky!*

I can't believe he's about to be my husband! Looking at the front of the aisle, Julie couldn't help but stare at her groom. *Handsome, smart, so understanding and patient… and he chose **me**!*

Being so distracted, the bride almost missed one of her favorite parts of the ceremony. Fortunately, her dad was paying closer attention and nudged her to stop beside the chair where her mother was seated. Pulling a single yellow rose from her bouquet, she handed it to Cathy and hugged her. "I love you, Mom!" Ron took his seat beside his wife and put his arm around her.

Turning to Meagan's chair, Julie took out a single coral rose and gave it to her with a hug. "I love you, second Mom!" Straightening back to her statuesque height, the bride completed the few steps left to join the group in front of the trellis.

With the couple lost in each other's eyes, they were barely aware of the minister speaking, much less what he was saying. When things suddenly got noticeably quiet except for the clergyman clearing his throat, they realized they had no idea what part of the ritual was happening. Tearing their gaze away from each other they both glanced sheepishly at the officiant, silently pleading for guidance.

"Hi," the minister whispered where only the couple could hear. "We're having a wedding here. Would the two of you like to join us?"

Stifling an outburst of giggles that threatened just below the surface, Anderson managed to reply, "Uh, yes please. That's why we're here."

"Wonderful!" exclaimed the clergyman, intentionally louder this time. All the guests chuckled as he continued, "Anderson, do you take Julie to be your lawfully wedded wife? Do you pledge to love, honor and cherish her, for better or worse, for richer or poorer, in sickness and in health, as long as you both shall live?"

"You bet I do!" the groom declared.

"Julie, do you take Anderson to be your lawfully wedded husband? Do you pledge to love, honor, and cherish him, for better or worse, for richer or poorer, in sickness and in health, as long as you both shall live?"

"I absolutely do!" the bride proclaimed.

The officiant continued, "Ladies and gentlemen, these two lovebirds have some things they want to say while they exchange their rings."

Julie handed Emily her bouquet and held her left hand out toward her love. He took her hand, slid her wedding band on her finger and said, "Babe, the day you popped into my life was the day that changed me forever. I can never thank you enough for letting me into your heart, for allowing me to love you the best way I know how, and for loving me so well in return. Today, you are making me the happiest man in the world by becoming my wife. I will spend the rest of my life finding ways to show my appreciation to you for that." He tenderly kissed the back of her hand before letting it go.

Taking Anderson's hand and sliding on his wedding band, Julie answered, "I am so blessed to have found you, Honey. We've had an undeniable connection from the start and have always had this groove where we just fit. It means so much to me how encouraging and supportive you are, and I will spend the rest of my life finding ways to be those things for you, too."

"Well, I think that's about it," the minister said. "Wait… am I forgetting some small detail?" He grinned at the newlyweds.

"You sure are!" Anderson said, and he didn't wait for permission. Wrapping his arms around his new wife, he gave her a big kiss, and everyone cheered.

"Oh, right… I knew there was something! You may now kiss your bride!" the clergyman declared. Nobody really heard him over the applause, so he waited for things to settle down before speaking again.

Once he had the group's attention again, he prompted the couple to turn and face their guests. With enthusiasm, he declared, "Ladies and gentlemen, I present to you for the first time, Mr. and Mrs. Anderson Blair!"

Chapter 22

Photos, good wishes, cake, and refreshments followed inside the house, then the Blairs bid their guests goodbye and set off on their honeymoon. With so much going on in their lives, they weren't interested in the typical lively destinations. Instead the newlyweds opted for a few quiet days relaxing alone in a rustic mountain cabin. The Fall colors they both loved so much surrounded the secluded cottage, and they spent their first evening as husband and wife snuggling in front of the warmth of the rock fireplace in the living room.

"How are you feeling, wife? You've had a lot of stress on you lately. You haven't complained once, which is admirable, but I know you must be exhausted." Anderson was concerned about her health.

Julie enjoyed a sip from a mug of cocoa he had made for her and replied, "It was a perfect day. Everything went off without a hitch, and the wedding was just as lovely as I imagined it would be." She put the cup on the sofa table behind them and stretched, then groaned involuntarily.

"I agree," he said, "but you totally avoided my question. Unless I should take that sound you just made as your answer." He put his hand on her cheek and turned her face toward him. "Look at me and tell me you're not in pain right now."

Sighing resolutely, she muttered, "I wish I could." Shifting her position trying to find a more comfortable one made her moan again, and she knew she wasn't fooling him. "You're right. I'm hurting. But I'm okay, really."

"How can you be hurting **and** okay at the same time?" Anderson was puzzled.

"It's hard to explain. I guess I'm getting used to it. It's a mindset. I know the pain is there, obviously, but I have to remind myself that the treatment is working, I'm getting better, and this current level of pain is less than I had before Doctor Jensen came along." That was the best she could do to explain it.

"Speaking of treatment, we need to get you set up and do your infusion. Sorry the day to do it happened to be today." When she started to protest, he shut that down right away. "Don't even **think** about suggesting you skip it. That's **not** going to happen." He stood and held out his hand to help her off the cushy sofa.

"Man, what happened to you?" she teased. "You sure got **bossy** when you became my husband."

"Hey, remember that whole 'in sickness and in health' thing? I take that very seriously. It's my job to help you get more of the 'health' and less of the 'sickness'." He grinned a non-verbal challenge her way.

"I guess I can't argue with that!" she conceded and followed him into the bedroom.

～～～

In the weeks after their honeymoon, Anderson got back to his work routine and Julie started focusing on preparing for the Lyme Awareness fashion show. She had wardrobe fittings and personal appearances associated with the upcoming event, so it was keeping her busy. Weekends the couple reserved for vegging out and enjoying their new home. They settled into a comfortable routine and found that married life suited them quite well.

A few days before the fashion show, Julie had a follow-up visit with Doctor Jensen. Anderson was unable to go with her, but she wasn't concerned because it was just routine. At the last minute Cathy asked to join her, so they decided to make a girls' day of it and go to lunch afterward. Emily was invited to go with them, but with Andrew's retirement drawing ever closer, she had her hands full learning the ropes at work and adjusting to being away from little Drew during the day.

"Thanks for letting me tag along." Cathy sat beside her daughter in the exam room. "I very much want to meet this doctor who has been taking such good care of my daughter."

"I'm glad you wanted to come, Mom. I want you to meet him, too. He's my hero!" Julie declared.

Doctor Jensen walked in just in time to hear her remark. "**Who's** your hero?"

"You are, of course!" she answered.

"Really? Well, thank you, but I'm just doing my job," he deferred.

"Oh, don't be so modest. You go far and above 'just doing your job' for your patients, and we all appreciate you." She wasn't letting up.

"You're making me blush." Turning toward Cathy he asked, "Who have you brought with you today?"

Holding out her hand, she replied, "I'm Cathy Chambers, Julie's mother. Her father and I have just returned to the area, and I wanted to meet the man who changed our daughter's life."

"I thought that was Anderson!" the doctor joked, and the ladies laughed.

Taking a seat, he became more serious and said, "I have the results of your latest blood work back, Julie."

She got a queasy feeling when he mentioned results. Lab tests always made her nervous. "Is something wrong, Doctor Jensen? You look so serious."

Brightening, he apologized, "Oh, goodness, no! I was up late last night with another patient, so I'm quite tired. I didn't mean to mislead you. Your results look very good! I've sent copies of all my records so far to Doctor Michaels for your chart in his office, and I have a set for you, too. You are progressing well, and I believe, at this rate, we will be able to remove that PICC line early next year!"

~~~

"Dad, is it okay with you if I take a lunch break?" Emily and Andrew had been steadily working all morning, but she felt bad for declining Julie and Cathy's invite.

"You don't need my permission," her father laughed. "You're entitled to have a lunch break, My Dear. Besides, in case you've forgotten, you're the boss! You can do whatever you want to do!"

"Let's not rush it, Mister," she chastised. "I'm not the Boss for a couple more months." She gave him a quick peck on the cheek and grinned, "But I like the sound of that!"

Watching his daughter head out, a thought occurred to him. *She's right. I'm still the boss, so I can do whatever I want to do, too.* Picking up the phone on his desk, he called his wife. When she answered, he turned on the old Peters charm. "Hello, Sweetheart. Would you do me the honor of joining me for lunch?"

~~~

Emily somehow managed to arrive at the cafe before Julie and Cathy did, so she got a table and instructed the hostess to have them join her when they arrived. She saw the two approaching and stood to greet them. "Surprise!" The ladies hugged and were happy to have the time together after all.

The waitress brought them glasses of water and after they all ordered the quiche for lunch, Emily jumped right in with the question uppermost on her mind. "How was your appointment with Doctor Jensen? Tell me everything!"

Julie squeezed a slice of lemon into her water casually and shrugged. "It was brief. I picked up my supplies, he checked my ports, just routine stuff. There really isn't much to tell."

"Oh, Julie, stop it!" her mother scolded.

"Whatever do you mean, mother?" the blonde was enjoying being coy.

Turning to the redhead, Cathy said, "Ha! She knows very well what I mean. 'Not much to tell', she says. Don't let her fool you."

"Oh, come on, you two!" Emily protested. "**Somebody** tell me!"

"Well, there was this one little matter of …" Before Julie could finish, her mother interrupted, unable to hold in her excitement any longer.

"She's doing so well, she can probably have the PICC line removed after the holidays! Isn't that wonderful?"

"Yes! That **is** wonderful! This deserves a toast!" Emily raised her glass of water and the others joined in. The three women clinked their glasses together as if they were enjoying the finest French champagne.

Emily declared, "I'm so glad I changed my mind and joined you for lunch!"

Chapter 23

"I'm happy you were all able to make it for this!" It was the day of the Lyme Awareness fashion show, and Julie was nervous, but excited. Her own parents, Nick, Emily and both of her parents, and Anderson had all shown up for moral support, and they were chatting with the model backstage before the show. Peterson's Place had even been granted access to have a camera crew filming the benefit and Karen was acting as reporter to cover the event for a future episode.

"This is a good-sized crowd!" Ron observed, standing at the side of the stage, and peeking out through the curtain. "It's quite a generous turnout!"

"Let's hope they have generous hearts and checkbooks, too," Julie whispered. "If this fundraiser goes well, it could make a really big difference."

"We're so proud of you for putting all of this together, Sweetheart!" her father bragged proudly as he turned away from the curtain and back to their group.

"Daddy, you're giving me too much credit. I didn't put **any** of it together. I just showed up when and where I was told to."

"Well, maybe not, but you were the inspiration that started the ball rolling, so you deserve at least some of the recognition." Cathy insisted.

"Your mother's right, so let us be proud of you," Ron maintained.

Raven dashed up to the small gathering breathlessly. "Julie! It's time to take your place. We're about to start!"

~~~

"Welcome, ladies and gentlemen, to the Lyme Disease Awareness Fashion Show!" Raven announced, then continued after the applause subsided. "When the designers and sponsors first approached me about joining with Black Raven Modeling Agency to host a benefit like this, I must admit I was surprised. I want to thank every one of you who got involved. I appreciate your willingness to see beauty and fashion in a different way, and to call attention to this most worthy cause."

The standing ovation caught Raven off guard, and she wiped a tear from her eye, her manicured red nails flashing in the spotlight. Quickly pulling herself together, she resumed, "And now, I invite you all to sit back, relax, and enjoy the show!"

Upbeat music started and the first model appeared. The statuesque brunette strolled along the stage decked out in a beautiful flowing red gown that was perfect for any formal occasion. She was followed by a lovely redhead who was stunning in a gold sequined cocktail dress, and next came a distinguished pewter-haired woman in a festive silver beaded pantsuit. Julie closed the formalwear portion of the pageant striding gracefully down the catwalk in a suit made up of black silk shorts and a matching blazer with a white sparkling camisole underneath.

The show continued in segments with the four models presenting designer outfits in the categories of sportswear, business attire and swimsuits. All the designs were well-received amidst much applause and admiration from the crowd.

When Julie made her final appearance at the conclusion of the event in a lime green dress with spaghetti straps, the crowd went wild. None of the other styles she had worn intentionally hid her ports, but they didn't exactly display them, either. The last gown, however, plainly revealed the PICC line in her arm and the port in her chest. It was a deliberate design in an obvious color, consciously saved for last to remind everyone what the occasion was about and why they were there.

After the presentation, people didn't seem to want to leave. The models, designers and sponsors all mingled among the guests, chatting about how much they enjoyed the event and what a hit the designs were. After a while, the sound system was turned back on and Raven stood mid-stage with a microphone.

"Ladies and gentlemen, may I have your attention, please?" Most of the group settled down at her request, so she resumed her announcement. "I'm glad so many of you have lingered because there's something I'm extremely excited to share with you! The numbers are in, and you have all amazed me with your kind donations!"

The room grew silent as the low buzz that had been underlying her talk ceased. "I am thrilled to say that your generosity today has raised over a quarter of a million dollars for Lyme disease research and awareness!"

The crowd erupted into a burst of cheers and applause. Julie could hardly believe what she heard. Her heart overcome with gratitude, she felt compelled to express her feelings. She made her way to the stage and Raven offered her the microphone. The people respectfully quieted again as she spoke.

"To say 'thank you' seems incredibly inadequate, but I don't know any other words to express the depth of my appreciation right now. To every one of you who came, who listened to our message over the past few weeks, who donated, or told a friend, or made a commitment to learn more about this awful disease..."

Her emotions got the better of her and the model couldn't say anything else. She lowered the mic and Raven put her arms around her. The other models made their way up on the stage and joined in the hug. The crowd began to clap and cheer again and finally the agent recovered enough to speak.

"I just had a great idea, and I hope you designers and sponsors will agree with me. I believe we should do this again next year!"

~ ~ ~

After the fashion show, Black Raven Modeling Agency became the talk of the fashion industry. Julie's career opportunities escalated significantly, and even the other models from the event had more requests start coming in for their talents, as well. The blonde had enough offers to work almost every day, if she could have.

It was all a bit more than Julie had been prepared to handle. She was still trying to catch her breath after the wedding and honeymoon, moving into the new house and getting it fixed up, doing TV appearances, and all the activity involved with the fashion show itself. She was a newlywed who didn't feel like she was getting to see her new husband very much, and that didn't sit well with her.

At the same time, she was afraid that, if she declined jobs, it would hurt her career just when it was taking off again. *Raven's been so good to me, and so patient through everything. And helping arrange the fundraiser, too. I can't let her down!*

On top of it all, as much as she hated to admit it, Julie was scared of having a stress-induced relapse of symptoms and losing the progress she had made with her treatment. One night at dinner, she finally decided to mention her concerns to her husband, and discovered he'd been having similar thoughts himself.

"I'm so glad you shared this with me, Babe. I've been feeling anxious about your health, but you always seem like you're doing great, so it's hard to tell when you may be taking on too much. I don't want to smother you or make you feel like I don't trust you to take care of yourself, but I do worry about you."

"Thanks, Honey, and I'm sorry for making you feel nervous, too. Fortunately, with Thanksgiving coming up in a couple of weeks, I'm going to get a little bit of a breather. That should help." She skewered a cherry tomato from her salad and popped it into her mouth.

"Uh, yeah, about that…" Anderson stammered.

"About what?" Julie asked.

"Thanksgiving," he replied, as if that word alone would clarify his point.

"What about it?" She still didn't understand.

"You mentioned to me that you wanted to host everyone here for Thanksgiving this year, remember? Maybe it's not the right time. That's all I'm saying."

"Oh, no you don't," his wife insisted. "This is something I've been dreaming about for weeks. It's our first Thanksgiving as husband and wife, my parents are back home, we have this beautiful new home… there is no way we're not hosting!"

"Okay, okay, clearly I was suffering from a moment of temporary insanity to even suggest such a thing!" They laughed out loud, then he sobered and asked, "Will you at least compromise and ask everyone to bring something so the whole meal isn't on us? I'm sure they'll be fine with that."

She considered his request, then answered, "Marriage is about compromises. Okay, beloved hubby, I agree to do that." She pierced another tomato and grinned.

Chapter 24

"That new husband of yours had a wonderful idea to do this as a potluck style Thanksgiving dinner," Cathy commented to her daughter as she put plates and silverware around the dining table. "This way, the whole responsibility isn't on any one household and everyone gets to relax and enjoy the day together as one big family."

"I agree, Mom, and I want you to know how much I appreciate you and Dad lending a hand getting things ready. I realize you've been busy getting settled back in. Anderson was determined to deep fry the turkey, which he's never done before, so he and the rest of the guys have been outside all morning, turkey sitting." Julie laughed as she put a dish of cranberry sauce in the refrigerator to chill.

Ron walked into the kitchen in time to hear the last part of what his daughter said. "That's probably a good thing!" he exclaimed, shaking his head.

"Oh, no! Dad, please tell me nothing's gone wrong with that fryer! The last thing we need today is a fire or some other drama!" The hostess wanted the first holiday in their new home to be perfect.

"Thanks to you having the foresight to thaw the bird and not put it in the fryer still frozen, we have a disaster-free experience, my dear." Her dad kissed her on the cheek then mumbled, "Of course, the fryer did almost tip over…"

"Daddy, what are you not telling me?" Julie was about to panic.

Laughing, he confessed, "Only that your husband and Nick are quite amusing to watch, Sweetheart. Everything is fine, I assure you. Relax, nothing is going to ruin this day. Not on my watch!" He headed back to the turkey roast like a sentry on patrol, making his wife and daughter burst into a giggling fit.

"What's so funny?" Emily arrived with little Drew, wondering what she missed.

"Apparently the sight of our husbands frying the bird is quite entertaining, according to my dad," the hostess explained. "Mom and I are staying as far away as we can, and I advise you to do the same!" Taking the infant in her arms, Julie snuggled him close and cooed incoherent baby sounds to him.

"When are you and Anderson going to have one of those?" Cathy prompted. "I know you will be great parents."

"I think so, too!" Emily joined in. "You guys need a little one so our kids can grow up together like we did!"

Gently handing the boy back to his mother, the blonde held up her hands in protest. "Hold your horses, you two. We are in no big hurry for babies. We've barely finished saying 'I do', you know. Besides, we're enjoying this new house, I just got my career back, I'm still in treatment… our plate is full for now, thank you very much."

"Speaking of full plates, this bird is officially done! When do we eat?" Anderson was clearly proud of his accomplishment, so his wife hated to burst his bubble.

"Everything else isn't ready yet, Babe. Why don't you guys go into the living room and watch the game while we finish up here?" She gave him a quick peck on the lips with a grin, then smacked his hand away playfully when she caught him stealing a marshmallow from the top of the sweet potatoes and stuffing it guiltily in his mouth.

"Yes, I would say my hands are full already," she chuckled.

~ ~ ~

Half an hour later, everyone gathered around the table. Meagan arrived with a festive bouquet of Autumn flowers for a centerpiece, and the ladies arranged the food buffet-style on the counters in the kitchen. Once everyone settled with their loaded plates, Anderson stood and picked up his glass.

"We want to thank all of you for being here today and letting us welcome you on the first holiday in our new home." He raised his glass, and everyone followed suit with cries of "here, here" and "cheers".

Their host continued, "There's a Thanksgiving custom of taking turns around the group and having everyone say something they're grateful for. I'd like to embrace that as a tradition in our home. To get us started, I want to say how thankful I am for my amazing wife. I still can't believe she married me!"

"You're too modest, Sweetheart," Julie teased. "I'm thankful my parents have moved back home. I missed you guys!"

"We missed you, too, Dear," Ron said emotionally. "My gratitude is for our daughter's recovery. I know you're still working on it, but you're making progress."

"Amen to that!" Cathy chimed in. "I'm thankful that you're so happy, Honey. Seeing your child truly joyful is the best thing a parent can hope for."

"Everyone knows our greatest blessing is this little guy!" Emily held Drew up and they all smiled as he wiggled and cooed.

"I'm grateful for all the people and friendships around this table," Nick added.

"Even you, Anderson!" The two men laughed, but they had become close as brothers, something nobody ever expected to happen.

"I'm thankful Andrew is doing so well," Meagan stated. It was a simple remark, yet it spoke volumes.

Her husband was the last to speak, and he joined Anderson in standing. "I, too, am grateful for **all** the things mentioned here. We've all come such a long way in recent years, and we truly do have so **many** blessings. There's one more I can add on a personal note, and that is, I'm glad to be retiring next month! Cheers!"

They all stood then, clinking their glasses together and generally saluting their good fortune. Everyone enjoyed the turkey and all the trimmings, then pitched in to clean up so they could adjourn to the living room for football and dessert.

~~~

"How are you feeling, Babe?" Even though she ended up with lots of help, Anderson was still worried that Julie may have overdone it with the family dinner. All their guests went home rather late, so by the time they were finally alone, he found himself overcome with a strong desire to protect her.

Where is this coming from? I mean it when I say she's the strongest person I've ever met. Sometimes, I honestly think she handles her illness better than I do. I guess I should be used to this by now, but I just can't help feeling protective of her when I see her in a vulnerable state. He moved to her side and took her hand, absently stroking her arm.

"I feel pretty good, Sweetheart. You worry too much." She appreciated all his caretaking and knew he was genuinely concerned, so she wanted to ease his fears. "I love how much you love me."

He laid down beside her and wrapped her in his arms. "If you think I love you now, just wait until tomorrow," he sighed. Closing his eyes, he snuggled closer and mumbled, "And the next day… and the next…"

Julie listened as her husband's breathing became steady and he drifted off to sleep. *How did I get so blessed? I always dreamed of a love like this but wasn't sure I would find it. As long as I have him by my side, everything else will work out.*

When she got uncomfortable and tried to shift positions without disturbing him, she wasn't able to and unintentionally woke him up. "Let me help you, Baby," he promptly offered, getting up and rearranging the pillows for her.

"Honey you don't…" She stopped herself. She was going to tell him she could do it for herself, then changed her mind. She knew her husband well enough to know that he needed to feel like he was doing something useful. Instead, she praised, "You don't get enough credit for how amazing you are."

Grinning at her as he finished tucking her in, he replied, "I don't know about the 'amazing' part. However, I think you do a rather good job of spoiling me with compliments, whether I deserve them all or not." Crawling back under the covers next to her, he continued, "Of course, I never tire of hearing those compliments, so feel free to dole them out as much as you like!"

Anderson quickly dozed off again, but Julie stayed awake a little while longer. She was enjoying her newfound grateful mindset, so she laid there thinking about how far they had come since they met. She was also happily looking forward to all the possibilities in their future together. Before she nodded off herself, one last thought went through her mind. *This was the best Thanksgiving ever.*

Chapter 25

"Is it really necessary to make such a fuss?" Andrew complained as he pulled his winter coat tighter around him. The December wind was picking up, making it a bitter cold day.

"Is it necessary?" Emily repeated. "No, of course not, but Dad, you know Mom is not going to let your last day before retirement and my first day as the new boss pass by without at least a little bit of fanfare."

The two had snuck away to do some Christmas shopping and were taking a break to warm up with cups of hot chocolate. Andrew pretended to be annoyed, but they both knew he actually enjoyed it when Megan honored him as only she could.

"There's no point in fighting her on it, and you know that," Emily reasoned. "We may as well have the 'if you can't beat 'em, join 'em' attitude, because it's happening."

His sour expression slowly changed to a triumphant one and he declared, "You just gave me a great idea, My Dear. We'll indulge your mother and let her throw her office party, but I think she deserves a bit of fanfare herself!"

"Dad, you look very suspicious right now. What are you up to?" Emily sipped the rest of her beverage and gazed skeptically at her father.

Gathering their packages and paying for the cocoa, he answered her with a grin, "Let's just say I need to add one more item to our shopping list!"

~~~

Everyone was once again gathered in the meeting room at AP Securities. As expected, Meagan's "little bit of fanfare" had turned into a full-blown party. She had lunch catered for the whole staff so there was a buffet line with sandwiches, potato salad, mixed fruit, and iced tea. Trays of cookies and brownies graced each end of the long conference table with a holiday-inspired floral arrangement in the middle.

The employees were understandably torn between the melancholy of saying goodbye to Andrew and the pleasantries of welcoming Emily on board full time. As the staff finished eating, Meagan spoke up before anyone could leave the room.

"Thanks for being here for the passing of the baton, so to speak. You've all been so wonderful to work with over the years. Andrew and I have enjoyed getting to know each of you, and we'll miss seeing you on a regular basis. We'll stop by from time to time to say hello."

"You mean to check up on how I'm doing, don't you Mom?" Emily quipped, drawing chuckles from the whole clan.

"Very funny, young lady," Andrew said, trying in vain to sound firm. "What I mean is, there's no need to check up on you. Your mother and I both have every faith in you taking over this company." Father and daughter hugged and the whole team applauded.

"Alright, let's settle down," Meagan spoke up over the noise. "I'm sure you're all very eager to get back to work…" She paused for the groans she knew would come, then continued, "There's one more order of business to take care of before you go."

A low hum could be heard through the room as Meagan reached into her purse and pulled out a small gift-wrapped box. She handed it to Andrew and said cheerfully, "We all chipped in on this together, so it's from the entire gang."

He sat his tea glass on the table and took the present. Stammering in surprise, he said, "I wasn't expecting this. The party was more than enough!"

Encouragement came from around the room and he looked from face to face.

"Open it!"

"Go ahead, Boss!"

"You deserve it!"

"Okay, okay… here we go," he conceded. Tearing off the gleaming silver wrapping paper, he discovered the box held a stunning, and rather expensive, wristwatch.

"Oh, my… this is… this is too much! You all shouldn't have," he stammered, unable to take his eyes off the exquisite timepiece.

"Don't be silly, Dad," Emily urged. "You built this place from the ground up, and you deserve to have something nice to show for all your hard work. Try it on!"

Reluctantly, Andrew removed the new watch from its luxurious box and took off the trusty mid-priced one he had worn for years. *I'm not used to such pricey things! But I sure don't want to insult anyone by appearing ungrateful for their generosity and thoughtfulness.*

Sliding the indulgent accessory on, he had to admit it looked good on him. It felt surprisingly good, too. *Maybe this once I can make an exception.* Holding his hand up to show off their gift, he exclaimed, "Thank you!"

When the accolades subsided, he called out that he had something to say. "I have a few surprises up my sleeve today, too! Remember, this party isn't all about me!" Pulling a gift bag out from under the table, he handed it to Emily.

"For me? You are a jaw-dropper, aren't you?" She was as puzzled as her father was a few minutes earlier. Once again, there were calls out from the group.

"You're the boss, now!"

"Open it!"

"Let's see what it is!"

When she reached into the bag and felt something wooden, she had an idea what it might be. "Oh, Dad, is this what I think it is?" Pulling it out, she turned and showed the staff the plaque that had been on her father's desk for as long as she could remember. Reading it aloud she said, "The buck stops here!"

"It belongs on your desk now!" Andrew hugged his daughter and used the opportunity to whisper in her ear, "Get your camera ready!"

Stealthily retrieving a small box from the inside pocket of his suit jacket, he held out his hand to his wife, who was standing off to the side, as she was prone to do. Taking her place next to her husband, she held his offered hand and looked up at him, wondering what else he had in store.

"Quiet, please! Quiet down, everyone. I have one more presentation to make, and then an announcement. Everyone who knows me is fully aware how I feel about this beautiful woman." He hugged Meagan closer to him and she blushed.

"We built AP Securities together, and while I tend to get most of the glory, the truth is, I could not have done it, and it would not be where it is today, without her."

More cheers nearly drowned him out, and he called for quiet again, then continued. "My dear wife, the best part of retirement is going to be having more time to spend with you. I could never repay you or thank you enough for everything you have done for me over the years, and continue to do now. I hope you will enjoy this small token of my eternal gratitude. I love you."

Feeling slightly uneasy about receiving so much attention, Meagan opened the box and was shocked to find a diamond-studded wedding band. She gasped at its exquisite radiance and had no idea what to say. All she managed was, "Oh, Andrew!"

Taking it from her, he slid the stunner on her finger and explained, "When we married, all we could afford was this simple plain band. You never once complained about it, but I've always told you that you deserved more, and someday I would do right by you and get you something better."

"This is definitely better!" She exclaimed as she found her voice. She turned her hand every direction and admired it, then finally showed it to Emily. Noticing her daughter didn't seem surprised, she narrowed her eyes and accused, "You knew about this, didn't you? The two of you were not Christmas shopping the other day at all!"

"We most certainly were!" Andrew defended before Emily had a chance. "I just made a little detour while we were out, that's all."

Unable to wait any longer, the employees pushed forward to gather around and get a look at Meagan's new ring. Everyone seemed to have forgotten that Andrew still had an announcement, including Andrew himself. Finally, Josie's curiosity kicked in.

"Boss Man, what did you have to tell us?" she prompted.

"Oh! That's right! In all the excitement, I almost forgot. My loyal staff has been very important to our success over the years, as well. In light of this special occasion and how amazing you all are, everybody has the rest of the day off… with pay!"

Cheers were quickly followed by goodbyes as the staff filed out. Then it was down to the three of them, just Andrew and his girls, contemplating the future.

Chapter 26

Seeing Christmas through a child's eyes, especially for the first time, is a joy beyond compare. Nick and Emily learned that firsthand, thanks to baby Drew. Even though he was only four months old, he was becoming so alert and seemed to love any kind of Christmas lights. He was learning to laugh, and that was the most beautiful sound the couple ever heard. Perhaps best of all, after enduring months of restless nights, he was finally starting to sleep through, and the family was settling into a happy routine.

On the first Saturday morning of December, the four couple friends met at Andrew and Meagan's to venture out into the woods behind their house and cut down their own Christmas trees. Everybody showed up early with saws and insulated bottles of coffee. Emily even had a little sleigh to tow bundled up Drew along on the big adventure. Unfortunately, when the outing was planned, they didn't realize it would turn out to be the coldest morning of the year.

"Now we know why we haven't done this before!" Emily said, her teeth chattering as their boots crunched on the frozen grass under their feet. She was thankful the baby had so many blankets to keep him warm in the sleigh.

"Whose idea was this, anyway?" Julie asked, wishing she had listened to her husband's urging and worn another layer of clothes and socks.

"Yeah, **Anderson**, whose idea was this?" Nick taunted, fully aware that the suggestion had been his own. *I'm starting to have second thoughts about this now, but at the time, it seemed like it would be fun.*

"Oh, stop your whining, everybody!" Andrew chastised. "It's really not that bad, and we won't be out here awfully long. Just wait until you experience the joy of picking out your own tree and cutting it down! It's an age-old tradition!"

"We're going to **feel** age-old by the time we're done!" Anderson attempted to lighten the mood with some humor, but everyone just groaned.

"Come on, soldiers, march!" Ron directed, picking up the pace and pointing ahead as if they were marching into battle. That did the trick and they all warmed up a little because they were laughing so hard.

Reaching their destination in much improved spirits, Cathy was first to marvel at the array of beautiful firs. "Oh, my, you were right, Andrew. This was worth the trek out here. Just look how gorgeous these trees are!"

Inhaling deeply, Meagan added, "Yes, and notice how good they smell! They are so fragrant. We knew you would love them!"

The group split off into couples so each twosome could find their perfect tree. Once their choices were made, the ladies stayed out of the way and played with Drew while the men took on the task of sawing down their selections. Somehow, before it was all said and done, the women ended up becoming cheerleaders, giving the guys the last boost of energy they needed to make their final cuts and wrap up the firs to drag back to the house.

By the time they got Andrew and Meagan's tree on its stand for them and were gathered around the fireplace to get warm, they all agreed the experience was a good one despite the cold. Several cups of cocoa later, they parted ways so each couple could take their own fir home to set up and enjoy.

~~~

Nick and Emily decided to have an open house mid-December. They wanted to enjoy the season with friends, business associates, and family members alike. Also, there were a few people who hadn't had the opportunity to meet Drew yet. The couple was so thankful for their little miracle, it was delightful to have any chance to introduce him to new people. Besides, after all they went through to cut down their live Christmas fir, they deserved to show it off to as many people as they could!

The food was ready, and carols were playing in the background just in time. Among the first to arrive were Doctor Michaels and Doctor Jensen, then Nurse Faye Gordon wasn't far behind. "Hey, it's like a Brentwood Heights Medical Center family reunion!" Emily exclaimed, greeting each of them with a warm hug.

Andrew walked up and joined them, having overheard his daughter's remark from the next room. "It's so good to see all of you under non-medical conditions!" He shook hands with each one then invited them to follow him into Drew's room for a peek at the baby.

"He's sleeping right now, so keep your voices down, but you have to come see my grandson! Wait until you see the Santa outfit his grandma got him. He's just the cutest…" Emily smiled as his voice faded away. *He's such a proud grandpa!*

Guests continued to amble in, and before long Josie showed up with a gift of cinnamon potpourri. She was followed shortly after by some other employees from AP Securities. "Hi, Emily!" Josie said. "Are you getting used to being away from the little guy now that you're with us full time?"

"Oh, I don't know if I'll ever be fully used to it," the new mom replied. "Let's just say I'm adjusting and leave it at that." The women chuckled, then Nick walked up and greeted the newcomers.

"Hey there, team! Come with me into the living room and check out this huge Christmas tree. I cut it down myself!" *Off they go, following Nick. The men in my life keep commandeering our guests!*

Mingling through the crowd, the hostess realized some of the appetizers were running low, so she headed to the kitchen to restock. She found her mother already there, arranging canapes on one tray and slices of fruitcake on another.

"Mom! You're supposed to be a guest today, not a hostess. What are you doing?" She knew her protest would do no good even before she said it.

"Don't be silly, Sweetheart. I'm here to help." She stopped fussing over the trays and looked affectionately at her daughter. "That's what mothers do."

With a quick peck on Meagan's cheek, Emily smiled, "Thanks, Mom. You're the best and I…" She was interrupted by a commotion at the front door. "What was that?"

"Let's go see!" Her mother carried the trays with her, dropping them off on the dining room table as the two women went to check out the noise they'd heard.

They reached the foyer just as Raven, Julie, and several of the other models from Black Raven Modeling Agency were crowding in. "Do you have a maximum capacity limit in here?" Charity asked with a laugh.

"It **is** getting pretty full, Em!" Julie agreed.

About that time Anderson and Karen managed to push their way through the front door as well. Before they could even say hello, Ron and Cathy squeezed in, too. Anderson took notice of the houseful of people and asked, "What did you guys do, invite everyone you know?"

"Yes, pretty much!" Emily replied, raising her voice above the music. "We just never thought they would all be here at once!"

~~~

The night after Christmas, Nick was rocking his son in the chair by the nursery window, enjoying the moonlit silence. All he heard was the sweet sound of the baby's steady breathing as he slept. When Emily's voice suddenly whispered beside him, it was all he could do not to jump and wake the little guy.

"It was my turn to get up with him," she noted. "Why are you out of bed?"

"Hi, Babe. You were sleeping so well, the least I could do was take your turn."

"That was sweet of you, Honey. We were up late with everyone at the annual Christmas Eve sleepover, and I guess all the holiday activities caught up with me."

"It's okay. You know I love these quiet moments with him," Nick confessed. "He drank his bottle like a champ, and he should be out for the rest of the night now." He kissed their son's balled up little fist affectionately.

"Sweetheart, sometimes I still can't believe he's ours. Just look at him." Emily took a seat on the floor and stroked their baby's hair.

The new Mom and Dad stayed that way for a long time, enjoying the warm cozy cocoon of their little family. Eventually they got up and laid Drew between them on their bed.

Nick whispered, "Merry Christmas, Emily. I love you."

"Merry Christmas, Nick. I love you, too."

Data Sources

Chapter 3:

1 "About Lyme Disease". lymedisease.org. Advocacy, Education & Research.

Accessed May 17, 2020.

https://www.lymedisease.org/lyme-basics/lyme-disease/about-lyme/

Chapter 4:

1 "About Lyme Disease". lymedisease.org. Advocacy, Education & Research.

Accessed May 17, 2020.

https://www.lymedisease.org/lyme-basics/lyme-disease/about-lyme/

2 "The Overlooked -And Deadly- Complications of Lyme Disease and Its Coinfections." Shea Medical. Accessed May 16, 2020.

https://www.sheamedical.com/the-overlooked-and-deadly-complications-of-lyme-disease-and-its-coinfections

Chapter 6:

1 "Climate Change Indicators in the United States: Lyme Disease". EPA (Environmental Protection Agency). Updated August 2016. Accessed May 16, 2020. https://www.cpa.gov/climate-indicators

2 "About Lyme Disease". lymedisease.org. Advocacy, Education & Research.
Accessed May 17, 2020.
https://www.lymedisease.org/lyme-basics/lyme-disease/about-lyme/

3 "Lyme Disease Transmission". CDC (Centers for Disease Control and Prevention). Accessed May 16, 2020. https://www.cdc.gov/lyme/transmission/index.html

4 "How To Recognize What Your Doctor May Miss-And How To Find Real Treatment". Shea Medical. Accessed May 18, 2020.
https://www.sheamedical.com/how-to-recognize-what-your-doctor-may-miss-and-how-to-find-real-treatment

5 Crystal, Jennifer. "Unraveling Spirochetes". Global Lyme Alliance. October 15, 2019.
Accessed May 17, 2020. https://www.globallymealliance.org/unraveling-spirochetes/

6 "Chronic Lyme Disease". lymedisease.org. Advocacy, Education & Research.
Accessed May 16, 2020.
https://www.lymedisease.org/lyme-basics/lyme-disease/chronic-lyme-disease/

7 "Chronic Lyme Disease (Post-Treatment Lyme Disease Syndrome). Healthline.

Accessed May 16, 2020. http://www.healthline.com/health/lyme-disease-chronic-persistent

Chapter 7:
1 Marcus, Mary Brophy. "When Lyme Disease isn't caught early, the fallout can be scary". CBS News. July 22, 2016. Accessed May 16, 2020.

http://www.cbsnews.com/news/lyme-disease-when-it-isn't-caught-early-fallout-can-be-scary/

2 "Treatment". CanLyme. Canadian Lyme Disease Foundation. Accessed May 16, 2020.

http://www.canlyme.com/just-diagnosed/treatment/

3 "The Overlooked -And Deadly- Complications of Lyme Disease and Its Coinfections." Shea Medical. Accessed May 16, 2020.

https://www.sheamedical.com/the-overlooked-and-deadly-complications-of-lyme-disease-and-its-coinfections. **Additional information from this article is in the addendum that follows.**

Chapter 9:
1 Klein, JoAnna. "Why Does Fall Foliage Turn So Red and fiery? It Depends." The New York Times. October 25, 2016. Accessed May 20, 2020.

https://www.newyorktimes.com/2016/10/26/science/leaves-fall-foliage-colors-red.html

Chapter 12:

1 Folbigg, RN, Lindsay. "FAQs About Caring for Your PICC Line." National Jewish Health.

March 1, 2019. Accessed May 23, 2020.

https://nationaljewish.org/conditions/medications/managing-you-medication-supply/faqs-on-picc-line-care

2 Jemsek, MD, Joseph. "The Jemsek Protocol™". Jemsek Specialty Clinic.

Accessed June 5, 2020. https://jemsekspecialty.com/treatment

Chapter 13:

1 Marcum, Lonnie. "Lyme SCI: The Dreaded Jarisch-Herxheimer Reaction." lymedisease.org.

July 31, 2017. Accessed May 24, 2020. https://lymedisease.org.lymesci-herxing/

Chapter 17:

1 Cameron, MD, Daniel. "About Lyme Disease: Overview of Lyme Disease."

Accessed May 26, 2020. https://www.danielcameronmd.com/understand-lyme-disease/

Addendum

Here is a group of symptoms that are associated with tick-borne infections and coinfections:

- **Cough, shortness of breath**
- Unexplained fevers, chills, sweats
- Cystitis
- **Fatigue**
- **Chest pain and heart palpitations**
- Cardiac irregularity
- **Double or blurry vision, pain, or floaters**
- Photophobia
- Hair loss
- Fever
- **Rash at bite site** or other areas
- Difficulty swallowing
- Swollen glands
- **Sore throat**
- Swelling around the eyes
- Unexplained weight loss or gain
- **Buzzing, ringing, or pain in the ear(s)**
- Difficulty eating
- **Nausea** or vomiting

- Diarrhea or constipation
- Tremors
- Eyelid and facial twitching or Bell's Palsy
- **Joint pain and swelling**
- **Abdominal cramping or pain**
- **Irritable bladder**/bladder dysfunction/Gastritis
- Testicular or pelvis pain
- **Neck cricks, cracks, or stiffness**
- **Joint or back stiffness**
- **Muscle pain or cramps**
- **Insomnia**
- TMJ (jaw pain)
- **Headaches**
- **Tingling or numbness**
- **Poor balance**
- Difficulty walking
- Seizure activity
- Stabbing sensations
- **Dizziness**
- Personality changes
- Mood swings/Irritability
- **Depression/Anxiety**
- **Confusion/disorientation**
- **Difficulty concentrating or reading**
- **Menstrual irregularity**
- Loss of libido
- **Trouble speaking**

NOTE FROM THE AUTHOR: The above symptoms in bold type are ones I have personally dealt with at one time or another on my own Lyme journey. Due to the lack of adequate knowledge and care at the time of infection, much damage was done in the interim between my infection and diagnosis/treatment. Consequently, many of these symptoms I still silently endure today. However, I credit Doctor Joseph Jemsek's diagnosis and cutting edge, God-given treatment for the level of recovery I have been able to achieve. This has resulted in the severity of my symptoms being drastically reduced, allowing me to live and enjoy a better life.

The vast amount of information that is available about Lyme Disease and co-infections could fill this whole volume and many more. The passages used in this book are only small portions of the details provided by the listed sources. If you would like to learn more about Lyme Disease, please check out these complete articles for yourself, and read them in their entirety. If you would like to find out how you can help join the fight, please check out **www.lymedisease.org**.

If you suspect that you or someone you love may have Lyme disease, I highly recommend you contact:
Doctor Joseph Jemsek
Jemsek Specialty Clinic
2440 M Street NW, Suite 205
Washington, DC 20037
(202) 955-0003
jemsekspecialty.com

Printed in Great Britain
by Amazon